Demon Hunters 3: Tainted

Demon Hunters 3
Tainted

Avril Sabine

Cracked Acorn Productions
Australia

Demon Hunters 3: Tainted

Published by

Cracked Acorn Productions

PO Box 1365

Gympie, Queensland 4570

Australia

978-1-925131-28-4 (Kindle)

978-1-925617-39-9 (EPUB)

978-1-925131-29-1 (Print)

Genre: Young Adult Urban Fantasy/Horror

For you, Cat. Since it's currently your favourite.

Cassidy is sick of her father looking for a miracle cure. He should accept there is none, instead of believing the lies told by those who prey on the desperate. But he doesn't and Cassidy finds herself in an abandoned industrial building staring into the flame streaked eyes of a demon. Only a thin line of salt keeping her alive.

*

This story was written by an Australian author using Australian spelling.

Name Pronunciation

Like many names there is more than one way to pronounce the following ones. These are the pronunciations used in this story.

Ibaelcaurzanon [ib-ail-cause-ah-non]

Iulia [oo-lea-uh]

Chapter One

Cassidy Wells dropped onto her bed, falling into the multi coloured pillows piled up at the bed head, staring at the posters on the wall opposite her. "I don't know." She held her mobile phone against her ear, twisting a strand of long reddish brown hair around a finger. "Dad's been working from home a lot lately, Amy. He's been a real pain about the slightest noise." It was getting harder to come up with valid excuses. She knew that eventually Amy was going to get fed up and stop bothering and she had no idea how to prevent that from happening. She let go of the strand of hair and it straightened immediately. Curls probably wouldn't suit her anyway.

"Aww come on, Cass. It's been forever since I've slept at your place." Amy paused. "Actually, I can't remember the last time I slept there."

Cassidy could. Very clearly. It was back when life

was still kind of normal. Eight years ago when she was nine. Before they'd realised what was going on. "I'll ask him."

"You say that every time."

"It's not like it's any fun having a dad who works from home. It's like living at his workplace." If only her father wasn't so determined to keep the promise her mum had pleaded with them to make years ago. No one would care. And after all this time, who was still in their life who'd known her mum before?

"Just keep pestering him."

Frustration arrowed through her. As if that would make a difference. "Amy I-" Her door burst open, interrupting her words. Obviously she'd forgotten to lock her door again. She pressed her phone against the bed. "Dad! How many times have I told you to knock? I could've been getting dressed or something."

Her father, Tony, who was almost six foot, looked like he needed to eat more and had dark shadows under his eyes. His hazel eyes, that matched hers, currently gleamed with excitement. Normally they were filled with worry. "Grab your bag. We're going out, baby."

Cassidy stared at her father for a moment, trying to remember the last time she'd seen him this excited.

A frown creased her forehead as she remembered the so called miracle doctor he'd found about a year ago. She guessed once again it would be up to her to be sensible. When she nodded, her father spun on his heel, closing the door behind him. As she put the phone to her ear, she could hear Amy demanding if she was still there. "I have to go."

"What's happening? Who were you talking to? Was that your Dad? Did you ask him?"

"I'll call you later. After I talk to him."

"Later tonight or later tomorrow?"

Who knew how long it would take to convince her father that it was probably only another person preying on the desperate. "Tomorrow." Weariness washed over her. They couldn't keep living this life. None of them. Somehow she had to convince her father to accept the inevitable. She didn't want to watch life pass her by as he chased after nonexistent miracles.

"Okay."

Cassidy could hear the disappointment in her friend's voice. She knew that feeling well. Along with anger, frustration and often wanting to scream at the world and demand why them. "Sorry, Amy. I will ask him. But I can't promise he'll say yes." She already knew he'd say no. Already knew it was going to be a complete waste of time asking him. Maybe she was more like him than she'd thought.

"Okay. I'll see you at school tomorrow. But ring me first thing in the morning to let me know. If I have to wait until I see you at school I'll probably die of curiosity."

"All right, I'll call you then. Bye."

She disconnected, dropping the phone onto her bed as she rose from it. Grab her bag? What did he have planned? Were they going far? And who was going to look after Mum? They never went anywhere together. Someone always had to stay home to look after her. Well, maybe not never, but it might as well be.

Cassidy strode to the mirror in her wardrobe door. Her lime green shirt and white jeans looked fine. Luckily she'd put off having a shower. She checked the time. After ten. What was he thinking dragging her out at this time of night? When he'd burst into the room, she'd expected him to order her to bed. She shrugged, grabbing her handbag. What did it matter? It was a school night and she was going out instead of being sent to bed. Whatever stupid idea he'd discovered, she'd deal with it. At least this would get her out of the house for something other than school or grocery shopping. Slipping her phone inside her handbag, she headed for the front door.

Tony was standing by it, jingling his keys. A plastic bag, bulging with odd shaped items, was in his other hand. "What took you so long?"

She put on her rainbow coloured sneakers, which had been lined up neatly by the door. "Where are we going?" Stepping outside, she watched him lock the door. "Is it far?" He only shook his head, remaining silent. She followed him to the white sedan parked in the driveway. There was enough light cast by the streetlight to see that her father was smiling. "Dad?" Again he shook his head and when he unlocked the car, she slid into the passenger seat. Usually she was the one driving the car. But only to do the grocery shopping. Never anywhere else. Life was slipping her by, something that happened to other people, not her. Actually, it was slipping past the two of them, just out of reach while they remained a prisoner of her mum's illness.

Tony waited until he was seated before he spoke. "You're never going to believe me. Let's just say I've found someone who can cure Sylvia. Prepare to be amazed, baby."

"Dad-" she broke off, not sure how to word her statement. It didn't seem to matter how many times she told him, and how many crazy people promised a cure that never worked, nothing could convince him that there wasn't one. She took a deep breath. "There's no cure for Alzheimer's. Mum will never get better."

His smile didn't dim. "Just wait and see, Cass. Wait and see, baby. There's no point telling you. This is something you'll have to see for yourself to be able to believe it."

Those words didn't reassure her. She eyed her father, unable to remember ever seeing him so excited. None of the other failed attempts had caused this level of excitement. It was worrying. And she worried even more when, over an hour later, they pulled up in front of an empty industrial building.

"Dad, I don't think we should be here. Whoever told you they can cure Mum wouldn't be at a place like this if it was legit." Outside the car the area was quiet and deserted. There wasn't even another car parked nearby. It was the sort of place that probably wasn't good to visit during the day, let alone at night. Her gaze scanned the area, finding far too many shadowy places for her liking.

"Come on, Cass. Trust me."

Chapter Two

Cassidy stared at her father, wishing she could see him clearer. But the only light that filtered into the car was from a streetlight well behind them. How could he even ask that of her? Especially after all the other times. "Who's watching Mum?"

"Sylvia will be fine. She'll sleep till morning. I gave her some sleeping tablets." Tony reached out and rested his hand on her shoulder. "I need your help, Cass. Things will be better after tonight. I promise."

She was tempted to ask him if he'd been drinking, but he didn't smell like alcohol. It was odd hearing him ask for help. He never asked. Told her occasionally, when it came to things like doing the housework and buying groceries, but never asked. It worried her even more. "Fine." Taking a deep breath, she swung the car door open. "Let's get this over and done with. But you owe me a favour."

"You're not bleaching your hair so don't bother asking again. No hair dye until you're eighteen."

"I want Amy to sleep over." She put one foot on the bitumen and was about to rise from her seat.

"Sure."

Her head snapped back and she again stared at the shadowy figure of her father, certain she'd misheard. "Really?"

"Really. Now let's get this show on the road."

She was speechless for a moment. "Even if this doesn't work? No matter what happens, Amy can stay over one night."

"It'll work, you'll see."

Yeah, sure. Just like all the other times. Hadn't he learned anything? Her gaze darted towards the building in front of them. Obviously not. "But if it doesn't work, you have to promise to let me have Amy sleep over, regardless."

"All right. If it'll make you happy, baby. Amy can sleep over no matter what happens."

Cassidy grinned. "Thank you." She leaned forward to drop a kiss on his cheek.

"Now can we go inside?" He gestured towards the building in front of them.

"Yes." Even though she was still worried about what she'd find inside, she couldn't help being happy about being allowed to have someone sleep over. Miracles obviously did happen occasionally. She slid out of the car, leaving her handbag on the floor under her seat. In a neighbourhood like this she didn't know if it was safest to leave it behind or carry it. But at least if she didn't look like she had anything valuable, no one had a reason to mug her. She waited for her father to grab his shopping bag and lock the car before falling into step beside him. "So who're we going to meet?" She scanned the area again, trying to see what might be hidden in all the shadows. It was impossible. An army of muggers could be hiding and she wouldn't know until it was too late.

"You're never going to believe me. You'll just have to wait and see for yourself." Tony draped his arm around her shoulders as they walked towards the building. "I can't wait to show you." He pushed a metal door fully open and they stepped inside. "Hang on. Let me get out my torch." He rummaged in the bag and a few seconds later a beam of light fell on the ground in front of them. He shone the light around, highlighting rubbish, leaf litter and dirt. "Not the cleanest place, but it has the space we need. And no one's going to disturb us here."

Cassidy shivered. And it wasn't from the temperature. Brisbane wasn't that cold in mid

October. "Dad–" she broke off when she saw the items he'd started to pull out of the bag. "Why've you got your fishing knife? Salt? Candles? What's going on?" Worry exploded through her, swamping the fear she'd felt on entering the deserted building. Not him too. Surely not him.

"You'll see." Tony picked up the two kilogram bag of cooking salt and moved towards the centre of the large, open, aluminium clad building.

"Dad?"

"It's okay, Cass. You'll see soon enough."

She wanted to grab the car keys and leave. Instead she watched as he made a large circle with the salt, carefully pouring it from the bag, the torch shining on the white grains as they fell. When he reached where he'd started, he straightened and surveyed the slightly crooked circle. Dropping the bag of salt, he picked up the candles and placed them in strategic spots around the circle, lighting each of them. The flames flickered, causing shadows to dance around the room. Cassidy hugged herself as she fought the urge to run. Was her father next? Hadn't this been one of her mum's symptoms? Doing odd things. Odd behaviours that they'd originally laughed off. No. Things like that didn't happen. One parent with early onset Alzheimer's was rare enough. But two? That had to be impossible. Besides, he didn't have any of the other symptoms. She'd have noticed. So what was going on? Maybe he'd finally cracked from all the stress.

"Dad?" She wanted to cross the room and beg him to take her home.

"Nearly done." He shone his torch on a handful of torn out notebook pages he held.

Cassidy took several steps forward but couldn't bring herself to cross the line of salt. She stared down at it. A narrow, unbroken line on the ground, a candle flickering nearby. "Dad?" Why wouldn't he tell her what was going on?

"Hang on."

She wished now she'd brought her handbag in with her. She could have at least checked the time. Or sent a text to Amy to tell her the answer was yes, while she waited for her father to finish having his mental breakdown. Anything so she didn't have to think about what was going on.

She didn't know which would have been worse. Meeting someone in this out of the way place or the fact they were alone. Alone and going crazy. She guessed it had to happen eventually, but why now? There were only a couple of months left until she finished year twelve. Couldn't he have waited until then to have his mental break down? She didn't think she could cope with this.

"Okay. Come over here." Tony stood in the middle of his salt circle. "Make sure you don't disturb the salt though. It's extremely important not to break the circle."

Cassidy took a larger step than needed to cross the strange barrier. "Are you okay, Dad?" He had to be. She couldn't look after two parents. One was hard enough and that was with sharing the responsibility. There was no way she could do it on her own. In the early stages her mum had begged them not to put her away, not to let anyone see her as she worsened. She had been terrified of losing not only herself, but them too. But there was no way Cassidy could look after her mum on her own. It would be impossible to keep that promise. "Dad?"

"Of course I am, baby." He flicked off the torch and placed it on the ground at his feet.

The numerous candles cast enough light to show the area they were in, but there could be anything hiding in the shadows around the edges of the building. "Can we go home, Dad?" Please say yes, she mentally pleaded with him.

He ignored her, picking up the knife to hold it in the same hand as the paper. The other hand picked up a fat, round candle that had been flickering on the ground at his feet. "Come over here."

Eyeing the knife she took several steps closer. "What's the knife for?" The sharp blade caught the candle flame, glinting in the light and sending splashes of light across the building.

"You don't have to worry about it." He stared at her a moment. "You know I love you, right?"

"Dad, you're starting to freak me out." Starting? He'd gone way past starting. Maybe it was time to go. Although where she could go to, she had no idea. She didn't even know exactly where she was.

"I'm sorry, baby. But you'll be fine. I need you to stay in this circle and no matter what happens never come out. Understand?"

She shook her head. "No. Not a single thing. What's going on? Really going on. And why are we here?"

"It won't be safe outside this circle, but nothing will happen to you if you stay inside it. Promise me that, okay?"

How was a bit of salt meant to protect her? She met his gaze, seeing the candlelight reflected in his eyes. What could she say to convince him to leave right this minute? She couldn't think of a single thing she hadn't already said. "I want to go home."

"Soon. Not long and you can go home, but I need you here so you'll know. You deserve to know the truth." He paused, the candle causing shadows to dance across his face. "I love you and your mother. Make sure you tell her that for me, okay?"

"She doesn't know who we are half the time. How can I tell her you love her? And why can't you tell her?" She could hear her voice rising and didn't even bother trying to stop it. What was he planning on doing?

Chapter Three

Tony glanced at his watch, wax dripping on the floor as he turned his hand slightly. "Midnight. He said three was the best time." He held the papers closer to the candle. "It doesn't say it has to be three. Okay, now this is important."

Cassidy could only nod. This wasn't happening. Maybe if she sat in the middle of the circle and closed her eyes she could pretend it was all a dream. Except she was wearing her white jeans and there was no way she'd be able to get the stains out of them from the dirty floor.

"Don't move from here until he's gone. I would and will do anything for you and your mother. You need to remember I love you both very much."

Cassidy nodded, since that's what he seemed to want. She desperately tried to make sense of what was going on. She'd been up since six that morning.

She wanted to go home to bed. Instead she stood there and watched her father read from the paper in his hands. She frowned, trying to make sense of his words. But they didn't make sense. None of them. They sounded like something that belonged in a horror movie. Crazy words that highlighted the fact her father had finally lost the plot and she was going to end up needing to take care of both her parents. She didn't think she could do it. No, she knew she couldn't do it.

"Ibaelcaurzanon I name you Remedy. Answer my call." Tony dropped the paper at his feet. When he used the fishing knife to cut his palm, the candle fell from his grip, wax splattering across the paper and floor. He stretched his hand outside the circle and let droplets of blood fall onto the ground, the knife remaining in his hand.

Cassidy gasped, her hands covering her mouth as she took a step backwards. Her gaze was caught on the red that was smeared along the edge of the blade. She wanted to grab her father and shake him. Demand what he was doing. Either that or run and never look back. Then it was too late. She couldn't have run if she wanted to.

A creature formed in the air near the blood drops. Shadows becoming a solid form. Skin rippled, a colour similar to Cassidy's hair, and dark wings spread out behind him. Black eyes that held the flicker of flame stared at them, then looked at the droplets of blood on the ground. His almost human face sneered.

"You would have me dine from the filth on the ground?" His deep voice was filled with scorn as he raised his head to stare at them in contempt.

"I… I was told… he said to… on the ground he said." Tony took a step backwards, nearly stepping on Cassidy.

She reached out her hands to cling to her father's arm. What had he done? She stared into the eyes of the man in front of her, trying to convince herself it was only the candlelight reflected in them. She didn't believe herself.

"Who said?"

"He was a man. But had eyes like yours. He said you could be the remedy. For my wife."

"Eyes like mine? Did he give a name this man?"

Tony shook his head. "No. I mean yes. I mean, not a name. He said four will see you caught. He has your name, the human to call and the means to end it all. I asked him what he meant, but he said you'd know."

"What is the time, human?"

Tony turned his wrist to look at the time. Blood

dripped onto his feet at the action. "Twelve-thirty. Nearly."

"What time did he tell you to perform this ritual?"

"He said three was best. But he didn't say it had to be three." There was a defensive note to Tony's voice.

Cassidy frantically tried to make sense of everything. But nothing did. Not one single thing had since she'd got in the car with her father. Maybe she'd fallen asleep talking on the phone to Amy. If that was the case then her mind was more screwed up than she'd thought. She continued to hold onto her father's arm, wanting to drag him out of the building. Only his warning that the circle would protect them was all that kept her from running.

The creature laughed. "You know nothing about demons, do you?"

Tony shook his head. Then nodded. "I know if you accept my offer you will have to do what I ask."

"What is your offer? And what do you ask?"

"My wife, Sylvia Wells, has Alzheimer's. I want her cured and healthy so she can live a long life. In exchange I offer myself as the sacrifice you need."

"No." Something finally made sense. Cassidy tugged at her father's arm. "No. Mum'd never accept that. Not your life for hers. Don't. Please, Dad, don't." Fear raced through her making her feel like her heart would explode from her body. "Please." He couldn't do this. She wouldn't let him. Her grip tightened on his arm. "Please, Dad."

Tony stared down at her. "You are never to tell her. This is between the three of us."

The demon's skin rippled and lightened in colour. His face became fully human, but his wings remained. "Between four of us. You forget the one who told you how to call me." The winged man nodded towards the paper scattered around Tony's feet. His eyes were still dark with flickering flames, but his narrow face and dark hair now looked human.

"Four? Is that what he meant? Caught? Is that some kind of agreement?" Tony patted Cassidy's hand that was still on his arm, his gaze on the demon. "Ib… Ibae… ahh." He stared at the papers scattered at his feet.

"Call me Remedy. That's what you want me to be, isn't it?"

Tony nodded.

Remedy gestured towards the paper. "Is that the only copy of the ritual?"

Again Tony nodded.

"Don't tell him anything," Cassidy whispered. "Please, Dad. Tell him to go. This is crazy." No, it was worse than crazy. But she couldn't think of any other word to describe it.

"Pick them up and give them to me. And hand over the knife."

Tony pulled away from Cassidy, who made a sound of protest. He gathered the scattered paper and keeping his hand within the circle, held them and the knife beyond it.

Remedy laughed as he took the items. The paper flared into flames the moment he took them and he let the ash scatter around him. "So you do know something after all. You can't stay in there forever. Not if you want to make a deal. You'll have to come out here if you're going to give yourself to me."

"You haven't accepted my offer," Tony said.

Remedy looked at the blade. He ran his finger across the side. Tony's blood coated his finger and he brought it to his mouth.

Tony gasped, staggering back from the edge of the circle. Cassidy reached for him, wanting to hold him in the circle and not let him go.

Flames leapt in Remedy's eyes and he nodded slowly. "You. Every last cell of yours will be mine to consume." He pointed at Tony. "In exchange your wife, Sylvia Wells, will be cured of her Alzheimer's. And it won't be an easy death. You had the insolence to use my name. The only reason I agree is you had the impatience to begin the ritual early. But she will never be cured unless you fulfil this bargain."

"It's a deal."

"Then step out of your circle and give me what I want."

Tony hesitated.

"Dad, please. Don't do this." Cassidy tightened her grip on him, pulling him into the middle of the circle. "Please, Dad."

"I love you, baby. Tell your mother-" he broke off, taking a deep breath. "Tell her I love her." He pulled away from Cassidy and stepped outside the circle.

She reached for him. But it was too late. Remedy drove the knife into Tony's stomach. He dropped to the ground, his eyes round, his hands reaching for the knife as a scream tore from him.

She echoed his scream, wanting to rush to his side.

Remedy's gaze fell on Cassidy. "Now you."

"No," Tony gasped, trying to struggle to his feet. "She wasn't the deal. You only said me." His hand tightened around the handle of the knife protruding from his stomach.

"I said every last cell of you. She comes from you. There are cells of yours that went into making her."

Tony tried to tug the knife from his stomach. He

gasped at the pain. His gaze found those of his daughter's, tears streaking his face. He wiped the back of his hand across his cheeks to remove the tears, leaving streaks of blood instead. "I'm sorry. I'm so sorry. Don't step out of the circle. Please. You have to-" he gasped raggedly. "Be safe. I can't-" he broke off on another gasp and gave up struggling.

Cassidy watched as he collapsed backwards, her eyes wide as she watched the blood spread around her father. Anger and fear filled her, both fighting for supremacy, a feeling of helplessness threaded through them. Her hands clenched into fists. She had to do something. She couldn't just stand here and watch him die. Nor could she step out of the circle and let the demon kill her.

The demon grinned. "Well? Step out here, little girl. I will make it swift for you. Surely you don't want to endure the agonies your father now endures? A second and it will be over and your mother will be cured."

"I'm not a little girl," she muttered. No, she would turn eighteen in a few months. Her gaze was drawn to the blood that continued to spread around her father. Although it looked like she'd never see eighteen. She was about to die at seventeen. Not to mention a virgin who'd never even been kissed. Well, not a real kiss anyway. A kiss from someone she loved and couldn't do without. A kiss from someone who thought you were their world. She swallowed hard as she thought of her parents. They had been each other's world. Until the Alzheimer's.

"I'm growing impatient. Two steps and you will be out of the circle. If you don't do it now I'll make your death last until nearly four." The demon moved away from her father to stand a couple of steps from the circle. He held out his hand. "Come."

"Stay in there," Tony gasped.

Chapter Four

Cassidy couldn't look at her father. Instead she stared at Remedy's hand. It seemed so normal. Long fingers, olive skin, human. Her gaze travelled along the outstretched arm, now encased in a black shirt, the wings gone. How could he be a demon? He seemed so human. Her gaze reached his eyes. Bottomless black pits. Flames. There was nothing human in them. His lips curving into a smile caught her attention. She hadn't even had a chance to live. How could he expect her to die before she'd even lived?

"Now. Don't make me wait all night." There was a sharpness to his tone.

"Cassidy, don't listen to him. I'm so sorry, baby." Tony's words were jagged, filled with pain. "I just wanted Sylvia cured. But not at the cost of you. Never. Just stay in there, baby. Please. Don't come out."

She gasped, her hand covering her mouth when she saw how much blood now pooled around her father. How much blood did a human body contain? She shuddered. There was no way she was going to die like that. Who would be there for her mum? Her mum! Her father wasn't the only one who'd given cells to create her. Cassidy's eyes narrowed. There had to be a way out of this.

Her father moaned, again trying to remove the knife. "Please. End this. Just end this. I want to die. Help me. Please."

Images flickered through her mind. Herself as a child, trying to ride her bike. Wobbling across the grass as she called out, "Daddy, help me." Her mum struggling to brush her hair and turning to her husband, "Tony, help me." It was never her father who was the one who asked for help. He was always the one offering a hand. Seeing him reduced to begging tore at her. She should have known her world would end the first time he'd asked for help.

Her gaze was drawn to the knife. It had started with that knife. The spilling of blood to make the deal. Her shoulders straightened and she met the demon's gaze. Her father needed her help. Begged for it. And there was no way she could let him die slowly. "How can I let him die like that? Let me end his life.

Then I'll step out of this circle. Let it be me. It's the least I can do for my dad." Her jaw clenched as she tried to convince herself she could do this. She had to. As long as she didn't think about it too much she was certain she could manage. Maybe. He continued to beg for help and she tried not to listen to the words that tore at her.

The demon gave a short, sharp nod and pushed her father towards the circle. He screamed as he stopped just outside the line of salt.

Cassidy reached out with both hands, wrenching the knife from his body. She was back in the circle before the demon could react. Bile rose at the sound the knife had made and at the sight of the blood dripping off the blade and onto the floor. She forced it down and met her father's gaze. "I love you, Daddy." She silently promised to help as he'd always helped her.

"Love you, baby." He closed his eyes, his hand pressed over his stomach.

She faced the demon. "He gave you the cells that were his. My mother's cells were not his to give away. It took two to create me."

"That is unimportant. Kill your father and step out of the circle. My patience isn't limitless."

Her hands tightened on the knife. She had no clue

if this would work, but she could think of nothing else. And she wasn't going to die willingly. There were still too many things she wanted to do. Like getting even with the one who'd tricked her father into calling a demon. "I bind my mother's cells within me to your life. While you live, so do I. When I die, so do you. What is done to me is done to you."

The demon laughed. "And how are you going to make that work? Where is your sacrifice?"

She smiled for the first time that night. A mirthless smile that bordered on a grimace. She emptied her mind of all thoughts. "Here, Ibaelcaurzanon." Her knife plunged into her father's chest. There was a moment of resistance before the sharp blade did its work. She couldn't look down. As long as she didn't think of what she'd done she'd be fine. Energy crackled along her skin and she let go of the knife. Her gaze stayed on the demon as she moved back beyond his reach.

"No!" The demon roared, trying to reach her across the salt. It was like there was a solid barrier between them. "You will pay for this." His tone was a low, threatening growl.

"I wouldn't make my life too miserable if I were you. If life weren't worth living I'd have to kill myself. And I'd be taking you with me." Her smile had no joy in it. Only bitterness. "And if I end up in jail over this," she gestured towards her father, still unable to look at him. "I wouldn't want to live."

"I'm not your lackey," the demon snarled.

"Aren't you, Ibaelcaurzanon?" It was time to see if her plan had worked. It wasn't like she could live inside the circle forever. She stepped over the salt, standing in front of him. She continued to hold his gaze, tilting her head to meet it, surprised she wasn't shaking with fear. All she felt was a kind of numbness.

The demon smiled slowly. "I wouldn't start feeling too pleased with yourself. It works both ways. What is done to me is done to you. By this you have made my enemies your own. And never use my true name. Anyone could be listening. Call me Remedy."

She ignored the lurch in her stomach, refusing to let him see how his words had alarmed her, trying to hold onto the numbness. But it continued to slip away. "How many enemies do you have?"

"Only two worth worrying about. And only one who knows my true name."

Inside she felt like a panicked child and the words 'oh crap' repeated themselves over and over in her mind. On the outside she kept the same calm in place that she'd needed so many times over the past eight years. "Then I guess we need to get rid of them." How hard could it be?

The demon laughed, throwing his head back. When his laughter ended his gaze met hers. "What do you think I've been trying to do all these centuries? I am powerless against a demon with my true name. That is the only one we really need to worry about. The other is insignificant in comparison."

Coldness seeped into her. She held herself rigid, refusing to give into the trembling that wanted to overtake her. "I suppose it'll be up to me to figure it out since you've already failed at dealing with him."

"Don't push it, little girl."

"That isn't my name."

"I don't care what you're called. Eventually I'll find a way to break this bond."

"My name is Cassidy."

"Well Cassidy, you better start crying and babbling about hooded men because the police will arrive shortly."

"What?" She glanced behind him, no sound or movement giving truth to his words.

"You didn't expect all this power that's been released would go unnoticed, did you? Hold out your hands so I can bind them."

She saw that somehow, while her attention had

been on the shadows behind him, the demon had donned a mask and now held a length of rope. "Why?"

"Because you don't want to go to jail over this."

She reluctantly held out her hands, her gaze falling on a black line with a touch of red in it that snaked around her left wrist. She frowned. How had that happened? However it had happened, heat flared in it while Remedy's hands were on her.

Once her wrists were bound, the demon ran a thumb over the line around her wrist. It wrapped around three times in a continuous, straight line. "Demon mark. Did you think you could do this without being tainted somehow? Now give me some of your blood. You left me with very little power to complete your request since you stole my sacrifice. Few people realise that for us the true power comes from when we make the kill."

She wasn't sure how this all worked, but there was no way she was going to let him get the upper hand in their forced partnership. "Give me some of yours first. I'm not your lackey either. We're partners."

The demon chuckled. "Don't forget you asked for this." A drop of blood appeared on his forefinger, as if it welled up from the pores of his skin.

Cassidy hardly had time to begin worrying before

the finger was pressed against her lips, blood seeping into her mouth. She gasped as she pushed him away with her bound hands. Fire coursed through her. She barely managed to stand upright, reminding herself over and over again that he couldn't kill her. Not without killing himself. When she could breathe again, she met his gaze. "I have nothing to draw blood with."

He reached down and pulled the knife from her father, pressing the point to her fingertip, his gaze holding hers the entire time. He let the knife drop to the ground and brought her finger to his lips. The flames in his eyes flared.

Cassidy shuddered, her gaze still caught by his. Her wrist burned and a sharp pain travelled through her body. She clenched her teeth, refusing to show any pain. The moment he relaxed his grip on her hand, she pulled away from him. "Now what?"

"You will throw yourself against your father the moment the police burst through the door. Sob and beg and do all those pathetic things humans do. I will race from the building and when the police ask, tell them there were three masked men that climbed into your car when you and your father stopped at street lights. They had a gun and made you drive here."

"I can't do that. I can't touch him." Not after having plunged a knife into him.

"You are splattered with his blood. You will do this." He reached out and ran a finger down the side of her face. "Rest here against him. Then hold him so your chest is against his wounds. You will mask the evidence. Do you understand?"

She could only nod. A crash in the darkness behind the demon drew her attention. She gasped as he pushed her to the ground and raced off.

"Stop! Police!"

She had never heard two more beautiful words in her life. She was safe. Safe. But her father wasn't. Her body trembled as she pressed her cheek against him. She knew it had been a bad idea. The moment she touched him, the brittle shell that had held her together broke. The tears started to fall and the pain she felt was almost physical.

"Dad. Oh Daddy." Her arms were stretched past him to get them out of the way and she tried to tug them apart as she threw herself across him. "Daddy. Please." Hands pulled at her and she struggled to escape. Her bonds were cut and the ropes fell to the ground. She tried to reach for her father again, but gentle hands pulled her away.

"You're safe. Everything will be fine now."

She tried to see who spoke but the world was a blur. She brushed at tears that fell harder as she felt the blood on her hands. Her father's blood. She shook her head violently. "No, it won't. Nothing's fine."

Strong arms wrapped around her and she let herself cry harder. All the tears and emotions she'd held back while she'd been fighting for her life poured from her. Then she was gagging and emptying her stomach. "Dad." She whispered the word and then thought of the ones she couldn't speak aloud. I'm sorry. I'm so sorry. She shuddered as she remembered the sensation of plunging the knife into him. She doubted she'd ever be able to forget.

Chapter Five

The next few weeks passed in a blur of questions and sympathy. The faces of strangers and familiar ones all carried the same expression, said the same words. We're sorry. Cassidy wanted to tell them she was sorry too. Instead she fell silent. If she didn't speak, those words couldn't escape. Her nights were filled with blood soaked dreams and she stopped attending her self-defence classes. Instead she spent hours on the internet, watching how-to shows on kickboxing and karate followed by videos on using weapons like knives and swords. There were enemies who'd seek her out and she wasn't going to rely on the demon to keep her safe. She didn't trust him even though their lives were bound together.

It took two months before the police stopped questioning her. And it was another month after that before she no longer expected them on her doorstep.

During that time, her mum was admitted to a nursing home and her family's solicitor tried to talk to her about where she'd stay. She spoke to none of them. Walking away to close herself in her room instead of answering. She ignored her phone, hurling it across the bedroom one day when it wouldn't stop. Emails remained unchecked and she rarely opened the front door. Eventually people started to give up, including Amy who she'd known since the start of primary school.

Even Christmas had passed with no celebrations and when she was notified her father's life insurance would provide for her and her mum she still didn't speak. She couldn't. The only words she wanted to say were 'I'm sorry'. Even her eighteenth birthday on the sixth of January didn't help. So she'd finally reached eighteen. She'd lived long enough to see eighteen, but her father wasn't around to help her celebrate. And her mum might as well be in a grave beside him for all that she knew what was going on around her. She couldn't even bring herself to visit her mum. It hurt too much to be reminded her father had died for nothing. His wife was still the same. Absolutely nothing had changed.

By late January she was still being woken most nights by blood soaked dreams. Each time she dragged herself from bed, dropped to the ground and did push ups. Wearing herself out until she could no longer think was the only way to return to sleep. Not that it helped for long.

"You can't fight them like that."

Cassidy was instantly on her feet, turning on the bedside lamp and reaching for the kitchen knife she kept under her mattress. As soon as it was in her hand, she faced Remedy. He leaned against her door, his arms folded across his chest. "What do you want?" It was the first time she'd seen him since the night her… she broke off that thought, unable to even think about it. Especially not straight after dreaming of it. She had no idea where he'd been all this time and didn't care. She didn't need Remedy hanging around to remind her of what had happened that night.

"I found some demon hunters to teach you." He pushed away from the door.

"I don't need your help." Her hand tightened on the knife. Nor did she want his help. Hate and anger filled her, replacing the guilt and sorrow that had woken her.

"You will take all the help I offer. I won't have you dead. Understand?" He stopped in front of her, his gaze meeting hers. "You might not want to live, but I do."

Cassidy forced herself to hold her ground. The knifepoint was almost against his chest. Only centimetres and she could drive it into him. But she couldn't bring herself to do it. She wanted to live. Turning away, she slid the knife back into place, her back to the demon. "I don't need your help. I don't trust you." She straightened, still keeping her back to him. He reminded her too much of her nightmares.

His hand on her shoulder turned her to face him. "I don't care what you want. You chose to bind us, now you live with the consequences. Get dressed and I'll take you there."

"How?" She eyed him suspiciously.

The demon laughed sharply. "Not with a click of my fingers. You'll drive your car. I'll direct you. Now get ready."

Cassidy shook her head. They'd expect her to talk to them. "I can't. I don't want to see anyone." It had been weeks since she'd seen anyone, months since she'd wanted to see anyone.

"You can and you will." Flames leapt in his eyes and he growled, "Get ready."

She knocked his hand from her shoulder with her forearm. "Stop bossing me around."

"Then stop sulking in your room. What have you to worry over? You still have an entire life ahead of you. A very, very long life." His lips curved into a smile, the flames in his eyes settling to a flicker.

Cassidy frowned. Was he clairvoyant? "How do you know it'll be long?"

"Because I don't plan to die."

It took several moments for the pieces to fall into place. "No." This time she did back away from him. She didn't get far. Her legs hit the bed behind her and she dropped down to sit on the firm mattress. She shook her head. "No. Impossible." She hadn't tried to do anything like that. She'd just wanted to live through the night and somehow avenge her father. She hadn't been thinking any further than that.

The smile became a grin. "Most people are overjoyed at the thought of living forever."

She struggled to form a clear thought. "Will I age?"

"Imperceptibly."

"How long will I be eighteen?"

"A very long time."

This comment brought her to her feet and she struck out at him. He grabbed her wrist, imprisoning it. "Damn you," she hissed. She stopped struggling, allowing him to hold her wrist. There was no way she could break free from his iron grip.

He let her go. "I was damned a long time ago by far better than you. Now get ready. I might have forever but that doesn't mean I wish to waste time on this useless conversation."

With one last glare, Cassidy turned and slid past the demon. She pulled clothes from her built-in wardrobe and retreated to the bathroom to change into black jeans and a black t-shirt. She looked down at herself. How was she meant to carry a weapon? She had no idea. The demon better not let anything happen to her until she could find a way to arm herself inconspicuously. Better yet, he could provide her with some weapons. She flung open the bathroom door and nearly ran into Remedy, who now stood in the hallway.

Her eyes narrowed. "You can't see through walls, can you?"

"Worried about your virtue, little girl?"

"I'm not a little girl," she muttered as she pushed past him. She rubbed at her left wrist, wondering at the burning sensation. She pushed that thought from her mind. There were other things to deal with. A glance over her shoulder showed the demon hadn't moved. "You will get me weapons. Ones that are easily hidden."

He smiled slightly as he started to follow her. "I will, will I?"

"Yes." A sharp nod of her head. "You can't be at my side all the time. I need something to protect myself with until you arrive." Hopefully she'd be able to deal with any danger without having to call him for help. There was no way she wanted to see him any more than necessary.

"There's some merit to your suggestion. I'll think about it. But right now we have other matters to deal with. You need to be trained by a demon hunter."

"Aren't you worried I might use what I learn against you?"

The demon laughed, the deep sound seeming loud in the normally silent house. "You don't strike me as being suicidal. Not after everything you've done to stay alive."

If he was talking about her father then he was wrong. That hadn't been so she could live, that had been because he'd begged her for help. Even to save herself she wouldn't have been able to do it if he hadn't begged her to. If she hadn't known that he was dead anyway. "You never know what the future might bring. Especially since it'll be a really long one." She glared at Remedy when he laughed again, sounding like he mocked her.

"I'll take my chances."

She fell silent again. Three months of barely a word and she'd broken her silence by having a conversation with a demon. She'd have been better off staying silent for all the satisfaction she'd gained. But he was the one person, if you could call a demon a person, that she wasn't tempted to say the words 'I'm sorry' to. No, she wanted to say 'I hate you. I'm going to kill you. Somehow'.

Chapter Six

Cassidy grabbed her handbag and automatically glanced towards the mirror. But it was impossible to see how she looked before she went out. She'd painted every mirror in the house with house paint when she could no longer stand the accusations in her own gaze.

She recalled the moment she'd been about to smash the mirror she'd stood in front of. Her father's eyes had stared back at her from the mirror, accusing her. But she hadn't been able to smash it, remembering how her mum had told her many years ago to be careful of the makeup mirror she'd been playing with. Taking it from her, Sylvia had returned it to her handbag warning her that she didn't need seven years bad luck. So she'd found some house paint in the garage and painted every mirror, crying the entire time as she tried not to meet her own gaze, barely managing to hold back the words 'I'm sorry'.

Turning her back on the mirror, she headed for the front door. Who cared how she looked? She'd lost weight, she couldn't remember when she'd last slept through an entire night and black had never been her colour. It always made her look too pale. Ghostly. She grabbed the car keys and paused in the open doorway, staring out into the night. It had been so long since she'd been outside. She took a hesitant step.

"Once it's daylight you're on your own. You might want to move a little quicker if you wish to prevent that."

"What happens at daylight?"

"Ask a hunter."

Cassidy glared at the demon for a moment, wishing for a second she had used the knife on him. Then she spun away from him, striding to her car. "Lock the door behind you." She didn't bother to look at him, just hopped in the car and turned on the ignition, waiting for him to join her. "Where to?" She continued to avoid looking at the demon, even when he sat beside her.

"Drive. I'll direct."

Cassidy mockingly repeated the words under her

breath as she reversed onto the road. She ignored the demon's chuckle as she headed forward. Great, now she was the entertainment. Anger rushed through her and her hands tightened on the steering wheel. She couldn't believe she was sitting beside one of the demons responsible for her father's death and wasn't trying to kill him. But he was right. She wasn't suicidal. And there was another one who was more at fault. Other than her.

"Turn left."

She felt the demon's gaze on her and ignored the urge to turn and look at him. Maybe it was a good thing she didn't have any weapons on her. She didn't think she could guarantee she wouldn't use them on him right this minute. How was she going to manage a lifetime of putting up with Remedy? A very long lifetime. She had no idea.

"At the least you should make eternity entertaining for a while. Just don't make my patience wear too thin. There are things worse than death."

Cassidy struggled to recall the words of her binding, but the night was awash with blood. It had overshadowed everything else. All she recalled was his name, the blood and her father's pleading. There was something she'd said, but she couldn't recall the exact words. No matter what had been said, she wasn't going to be submissive. Forever was a very long time. She opted for bravado. "I guess you better heed those words too."

He nodded his head. "Turn." He gestured towards the direction.

Silence fell between them, broken only by directions until the demon said, "Pull up in front of that house." He pointed to a spacious timber house nestled amongst flowering gardens. It was painted in neutral creams and browns with white backed curtains at the windows. The place was dark, only the streetlight providing any light.

Cassidy reluctantly pulled up and made her way to the front door. Did he really expect her to knock on someone's door after midnight when they were probably sleeping? She glanced towards him. It looked like it. She hesitantly knocked, the sound seeming week and pathetic. Her next knock was louder.

"All right. I'm coming. Quit with the banging," an irate voice called from inside before the door was flung open.

She eyed the young man framed by the doorway. He had extremely short, sandy blond hair. Green eyes stared at her intensely and he had to be over six foot.

She noticed he absently rubbed at a mark similar to hers on his wrist. His only went around twice.

The young man slowly smiled. "Well hello, bad influence. You took your time in finding your way to me. And they thought leaving me here would get me away from all bad influences."

"You're not here to lose your virginity, quit ogling him."

Cassidy turned on the demon, masking her embarrassment with anger. "Ogling? No one says words like that anymore. And I wasn't ogling him. I was thinking. Why don't you talk to him if you're so worried about wasting your valuable time?"

Another young man joined the first one in the doorway, nearly as tall. He also had very short sandy blond hair but with a little more length at the front. At his throat was a gold cross on a leather cord and he had a silver stud, in the shape of a cross, in one ear. His demon mark went just over twice around his wrist. His warm brown eyes fell on Cassidy before they went back to the young man in the doorway. "Who's this, Gabe? Not one of your friends from Sydney, is it?"

Gabe grinned. "I have no idea Riley, but I'm hoping she's going to disagree with the demon about why she's here." He held out his hand. "I'm Gabe Hunter. And you are?"

She took his hand. "Gabe? As in Gabriel? The angel?"

"Don't start," Gabe muttered.

The demon brushed her aside to stand in front of the young men. "Demon hunters, train this girl to kill demons."

Riley laughed. "Now I've heard everything. Why would a demon want a human taught how to kill demons?"

Remedy's gaze narrowed, flames leaping higher in his eyes. "You will refrain from meddling in my business. Train the girl. That's all you need to do."

Riley's laughter disappeared. "We don't take orders from demons. The girl can stay if she needs our help, but you aren't welcome here."

Remedy grabbed Cassidy's arm, forcing her to meet his gaze. "Our business is to remain exactly that. I will collect you an hour before dawn. If you're not ready you'll have to find your own way home." He released her before she could speak and disappeared into the night.

Gabe stared after Remedy for a moment, then stepped out of the doorway. "You might as well come in. No point standing out here for what's left of the night."

Cassidy looked from one to the other, then glanced in the direction Remedy had taken off in. "I don't know. I think maybe I should head home."

"You're lucky you can go home," Gabe muttered.

"Do you want me to wake my grandmother?" Riley asked.

"You live with your grandma?"

Riley grinned. "She's actually my great grandmother. And no, not usually. But I'm here babysitting him." He nodded towards Gabe.

"I didn't ask my mum to ditch me here after Charlotte's wedding. It's not like I've got any way to get home. I can't walk to Sydney from Brisbane. Although I have been tempted. And it's a bit hard to get a job when you've got no references." He looked pointedly at Riley.

Riley took a step back, holding up his hands as if to protect himself. "I'm not about to interfere. Your mum'd kill me."

"No she wouldn't. That's a sin. And we all know that sin must be eradicated." There was bitterness in Gabe's voice.

"So maybe she wouldn't kill me, but I'd probably wish she had by the time she was finished with me."

Cassidy shook her head with a frown. There was already enough craziness in her life. She didn't need any more. "Nice meeting you pair, but I think I'll be going now." She waved with her left hand. Feeling the demon mark writhe on her skin as her hand came close to the house.

Gabe grabbed her arm, tugging her forward to watch the marks twitch and turn like snakes slithering across her skin. "That can't be good."

Riley stared too. "Maybe we should wake Gran."

Gabe continued to hold her arm, even though she tried to tug it away. "She's tainted, isn't she?"

Riley nodded.

"Let go of me," Cassidy said between gritted teeth.

"What deal did you make with him?" Gabe released her arm.

Cassidy took a step backwards. "That's none of your business." She wasn't about to spill all her secrets. Spilling her father's blood had been bad enough. There was no way she was going to discuss it.

"Does he think we can help?" Riley asked.

"Who?" Cassidy frowned again.

"Your demon," Gabe said.

"He's not my demon." At least she didn't think so. Did she own him in some kind of way because of the ritual she'd performed? "Look, I'm going. You don't need to worry about any of this. I haven't got a clue why Remedy brought me here."

"I'm guessing it wasn't to train you to kill him," Riley said.

"I bet there's another demon involved somehow," Gabe said.

Riley nodded. "There'd have to be. But why a human? It'd make more sense if he'd enlisted another demon to help him."

Cassidy took a step backwards. "Like I said, it was nice meeting you."

Gabe turned away from his discussion with Riley and stepped forward, placing a hand on her back so she couldn't retreat further. "Whoa, not so fast. Demons don't like to be ignored. Are you in any danger from him? Do you need help getting rid of him?"

Fear skittered through her. "No! You can't."

"Why not," Riley asked.

"Because…" her voice trailed off and she rubbed at her demon mark.

Gabe swore. "Don't tell me you bound yourself to him. What if he takes over your body? Did you ever think about that?"

Cassidy's legs began to tremble and she desperately needed to sit down before they gave out. "He can do that?" Her voice sounded unnaturally small. No, lost was the word and that was exactly how she felt. Lost, alone and scared. She didn't like the feeling one bit.

Riley stepped to her other side. "Come on." He cupped her elbow. "Come inside and sit down. We'll figure out what he can do."

Chapter Seven

Shaking her head, Cassidy allowed herself to be led inside. There was no way she was going to tell them everything that had happened. She couldn't even think about it let alone talk about it. It was bad enough reliving it each night in her dreams. She was led into a lounge room off the foyer, to her right, and collapsed into the first armchair. "Do you have to tower over me?"

Gabe sat across from her while Riley retreated to the doorway. He glanced behind him. "Maybe I should wake Gran."

"Grow some balls, Riley. Cut the apron strings and make your own choices for a change," Gabe growled.

Riley crossed his arms over his chest and leaned against the door frame with a chuckle. "Like you? You're still here, aren't you? I bet if you really tried you could find a way home to Mummy."

Gabe leapt to his feet, his hands becoming fists. "It's only been two days."

Cassidy instantly jumped to her feet too. "That's it. I'm out of here. You pair can smash each other's faces in for all I care."

Gabe held a hand out in front of her like a barricade. "Stay. Our fight can wait. What did you do to earn yourself a best friend like your flame loving mate who left you here?"

"I was trying not to get myself killed."

Riley crossed the room dropping into a chair. "All right. Let's all sit down and figure this out. I'm sure something can be done about the problem. Now what happened?"

Cassidy stared down at him. No way in hell was she telling him anything. She shook her head. "I can't."

"What if we start with when?" Riley asked.

"When?" Cassidy looked at him blankly.

"When." Riley grinned at her. "As in when did the incident occur? Well gee officer, it was a dark and stormy night last week."

Cassidy couldn't return the grin. "October." Even saying the month brought the scent of blood to her. "The fifteenth of October." She would never be able to forget that date. Dropping back into the chair, she watched as Gabe returned to his. "Last year."

"Not good," Gabe said.

Riley nodded. "So what's changed that he's brought you to us now?"

Cassidy shrugged. "He said he found some hunters to teach me."

Gabe shook his head. "That's not it. Demons know we're here. We're like a beacon to all the hell dwellers." He tapped his demon mark. "Just like we can feel them, they can feel us nearby."

Cassidy rubbed at her mark, which was still moving lazily under her skin. "Is that why it burns?"

"The more it burns the stronger the demon," Riley said. "But it shouldn't move like that. You must be part demon. How did you do it? It'd take more than just his blood."

Cassidy shook her head. I'm sorry. I'm so sorry. She closed her eyes as her fingers wrapped around her wrist and she took a deep, shaky breath, refusing to let the words escape. She opened her eyes and blinked back the vision of blood.

Gabe leaned forward in his chair. "What's your name? I've been told calling someone girl isn't very nice. More like what a demon would do."

"Cassidy. Cassidy Wells."

"We can't help you unless you tell us what the problem is." Gabe reached out to unwrap her hand from around her wrist, clasping it in his. "Look around you. These bookcases contain books on demons and how to deal with them. Our family has been getting rid of demons for centuries."

Cassidy looked around the spacious room. A floor to ceiling built-in bookcase covered the wall opposite the door, crammed with books behind its glass doors. She had never seen so many books in one place outside a bookstore or library. The rest of the room was filled with a pale brown lounge suite, a rustic coffee table, a couple of large square footstools and a long display cabinet filled with ornaments and framed photos. "Can I read them?"

"We can start you off with the basic manual." Riley rose to his feet and opened the furthest glass door, pulling out a paperback book. "My great, great grandfather wrote it."

Cassidy took the book and stared at the title. Demonology by Patrick Hunter. The demon on the cover looked like a demon. The face was pure evil and he had five short horns on each side of his arms starting from his shoulders and becoming progressively smaller as they went down his arms.

"Why doesn't Remedy look like this?" She tapped the picture.

"Some demons can take two forms. Their natural form and a human like form. But some demons look human naturally," Riley said.

"So I could walk past a demon and not even know?"

Gabe shook his head. "You'd know." He pointed to her wrist. "Your demon mark would let you know."

"But before this, I wouldn't have known?" Surely not. People would have to notice demons, no matter how human they appeared.

"Welcome to the world of demons. No more fun for you and sinning is definitely out." Gabe's voice was filled with bitterness.

"What do you mean?" Cassidy looked from Gabe to Riley. "There are rules I have to live by?" Why hadn't anyone warned her? She was not good at following rules.

Riley shot a dark look at Gabe. "Don't listen to him. He's mad at everyone for something someone else did. Look, why don't you take that book with you and read it. I'll give you my phone number and you can call me if you have any questions."

Gabe rose to his feet. "How about I give you my number instead and we can go out and complain about how demons screw up your life. Or better yet, are you over eighteen?" When she nodded, he continued, "Then how about we forget all about demons and go nightclubbing this weekend."

"How about you both keep your numbers and I get out of here." Still clutching the book, Cassidy headed for the door.

Before she could open it, Gabe reached her, his hand wrapping around her upper arm. "Sorry." He dropped his voice. "Riley's right, but don't you dare tell him I said so." He glanced over his shoulder. Riley wasn't in the foyer. "Take his number and call him when you've got a question. Demons aren't something to mess around with. People usually end up dead when they have dealings with them."

The word dead brought to mind her father. As if she needed any more reminders. She pulled out of his grip. "I don't need help from either of you."

Riley strode into the foyer, holding out a piece of paper. He grinned. "Both our numbers." When his phone rang, he pushed the paper at her. "Go on. Take it." When she did, he answered his phone. "I know, I know… shortly… we had an interruption…was it a demon disturbance?" He closed his phone with a chuckle and turned to Gabe. "Time to go hunting."

"Hunting?" Cassidy stared at Riley. "You're demon

hunters." It all fell into place. "I want to hunt demons with you."

"Oh, no you don't." Gabe shook his head. "No way in hell. You're not ready."

"I didn't ask you." Cassidy turned from Gabe to Riley. "I asked you."

"Same answer, sweetheart." Riley reached out and tapped the edge of the book. "Do a little study, pass your exams and I'll think about letting you come along."

"There's a hunter exam?" Cassidy's frown became a glare when Gabe laughed. "Fine." She spun on her heel. "I don't need either of you anyway." She'd figure out how to hunt them on her own.

"Thanks a lot, Gabe." Riley hurried forward and placed his hand on the front door before she could open it. "It was a figure of speech. I wasn't teasing you. Ignore Gabe. And call me when you get to the end of that book." He smiled at her. "I'll let you borrow another one."

"I'll think about it." She pointedly looked at his hand. When he moved it she opened the door and stepped outside. It was still night and Remedy was nowhere in sight. She turned to stare at Gabe and Riley. Words tumbled through her mind. Not a single one seemed right. Instead she turned again, without speaking a word, and walked to her car. Sitting in the driver's seat, she stared at the two hunters who remained at the front door, watching her.

Not knowing what else to do, she started the car and headed for home. She was nearly there when Remedy appeared in the passenger seat, causing her to swear and nearly drive off the road. "Don't do that again."

"You'll have to be more specific. Do what?"

"Just appear like that. What are you trying to do? Get me killed?"

"Killed? Not even close. Were the hunters of use?"

Cassidy shrugged as she pulled up in front of her home. "I don't know. They gave me a book to read."

Remedy looked at the book, which sat between the two seats on the centre console, and chuckled. "Some things never change. They've been using this book for decades. At least Patrick knew what he was doing. And he was an interesting man to talk to."

Cassidy stared at him, her mouth open, glad she was no longer driving.

"Close your mouth, girl. It makes you look like an idiot."

She closed her mouth with a snap. "You knew him?"

"Of course I knew him. Are you going to sit in your car all night? If you plan to spend this much time in it, I suggest buying a larger one. Something more comfortable."

Cassidy grabbed the book and hopped out of the car, slamming the door behind her before striding inside. When Remedy followed she turned to him with a glare, her finger pointing at him. "Stop following me and stay out of my house."

Remedy stilled. The air crackled around him. "If they told you to get your house blessed, then you better think again. You are never to bar me from your house. Understand?"

Cassidy felt fear at the look in Remedy's eyes. She held his gaze, forcing her voice to remain steady. "If you can enter then what about other demons? You can't always be here." At least she hoped he couldn't. She didn't want a demon living with her permanently. And particularly not this one.

"Salt across all the entrances. Put one of my feathers in the middle of the salt you cover your bedroom window ledge with. I'll be able to cross that line only. The salt must be continuous and unbroken. That will keep the minor demons out during the day when I can't be here to protect you."

"What about the major demons?"

"Didn't the hunters teach you anything? Major demons can't roam in the day."

Cassidy felt like growling in frustration. "Will they be able to cross the salt lines?"

"No. But I can be with you of a night."

"Isn't that the answer to all my prayers?" Cassidy's tone was heavily laced with sarcasm.

Remedy's lips curved into a smile as he drew closer. "Prayers aren't what bring us." He drew her left hand to him, breathing in the scent of her wrist near the demon mark. "Blood brings us forth." His grip tightened on her when she started to draw away.

Cassidy continued to meet his gaze, refusing to look elsewhere. "I'll remember that." Flames flickered in his dark eyes and she had to remind herself to breathe. To remain still and keep breathing.

Remedy stared at her a moment longer before he nodded once, released her then turned and walked away.

Chapter Eight

Cassidy watched him go then swore when she realised she'd forgotten to ask him why he'd chosen now to take her to the demon hunters. She made a mental note to ask him next time she saw him, then headed to bed with her book. She read until she fell asleep, waking to find the book on the floor beside her and her bedside light still on. After using the bathroom she returned to her bed, finally dragging herself out of bed late afternoon once she'd finished reading the book.

Heading for the kitchen, she poured herself a bowl of dry Nutri-Grain and picked them from her bowl one at a time as she thought over what she'd read. She had a million questions, but she wasn't going to ring the hunters. Patrick had far too many rules and believed in all sorts of religious stuff. No wonder Gabe complained about not sinning. The poor guy had probably been raised on this crap and hadn't been allowed to enjoy life at all. Not for her. No way. She'd figure out her own way of doing things. But first she needed salt.

She pushed the bowl of cereal aside. And some decent food. There wasn't much left in the house and she was down to the last of the meals people had made her, during the early weeks, and shoved in the freezer when she wasn't interested in eating.

After a shower, Cassidy stared at the handful of clothes still in her wardrobe. She'd thrown out everything except her black clothes and she'd never had very many of them. But every other colour had seemed drenched in blood. An image of her white jeans came to mind and she pushed it aside. She'd had to burn them. During the early days, the world had seemed drenched in blood. Nights had been safer. And black, well black didn't show blood so easily. She'd been able to look at it without seeing large puddles of blood spreading across it.

Dressed in a pair of black shorts and a shirt, she grabbed her handbag and headed for the car. She eyed the passenger seat. New transport too. A motorbike. Remedy could find his own way around. She wasn't his chauffeur. Cassidy's eyes closed momentarily as thoughts of motorbikes brought back memories of being on the back of her father's motorbike when she was a kid. It had been those memories that had convinced her to learn how to ride one. She forced the memories away before they brought tears. She'd shed a lifetime of tears in the past few months.

She had to stay strong. There was no one but a demon to look out for her and she was damned if she'd ask him for more help than she needed to. Damned. According to Patrick Hunter she probably was. Well he could keep his religion because there was no way she was going to hell or living by his narrow beliefs.

Cassidy started the car and headed for the supermarket, arriving as night fell. Walking inside she was hit by the noise of humanity. It took all her willpower to move forward rather than run to the safety of her car. Salt. She had to get salt. Maybe a little food. But salt was the most important item.

Each step forward was an agony. She saw her father's favourite aftershave was on special, there was a shirt like one he'd bought a year ago and when she reached for a jar of coffee it was to automatically pick his usual flavour. Her hand closed into a fist before she could grab the jar.

"They say it's bad for you, but you only live once, right?"

Cassidy turned to see a guy grinning at her, one hand on a hip. She could only nod when all she really wanted to do was tell him to leave her alone. Once she would have been flattered to have a good looking guy strike up a random conversation with her.

"Go on, you know you want a jar." His grin stayed in place as he lowered his voice and leaned closer. "I won't tell anyone."

Remedy slipped up beside her and draped an arm around her shoulders as he reached for a different jar. "This one, baby."

She tensed at hearing her father's name for her on his lips. Before she could speak, his grip tightened on her shoulder.

The guy chuckled. "Guess you didn't need any help after all." He shrugged. "It's always the way." With a grin and a nod he strode away.

Remedy bent his head so his lips brushed against her ear. "I own you. No other can have you."

Fear fought with anger. She kept her voice low, glad their end of the aisle was momentarily empty of shoppers. "It's the other way around. I own you."

"It's the same. You're mine. Don't even think about a boyfriend. They won't live a second beyond the moment they put a hand on you." His lips twisted into a mocking smile. "That shouldn't worry you.

Haven't you pushed everyone away since we met? You don't want to get close to anyone. That involves letting yourself care."

She glared at him, biting back the angry words she wanted to shout. Instead she spun away, leaving her trolley in the aisle. She almost reached the exit when she remembered the salt. It was bad enough having one demon in her house, she didn't want to leave it open for any who wandered by. She turned and saw Remedy waiting at a checkout for her, with the trolley. Her jaw clenched as she strode back to him, ignoring his smile when she reached his side. She kept her gaze on the handful of groceries and the two bags of salt in the trolley.

"I knew you'd be back, baby."

Cassidy's hands tightened into fists. She bit back her anger and waited to be served. Once they were home she'd tell him what she thought about his choice of words. Not here. It was bad enough being surrounded by so many people without having all their attention on her.

They were scarcely in the front door when Cassidy turned on him to yell. She jumped back, dropping the bags of groceries as his wings unfurled behind him, his shirt missing. She gaped, shutting her mouth quickly as she recalled his comment on that habit. Her eyes narrowed. "What's going on?"

Remedy reached up and removed a feather from his wings. "Don't forget to use this when you salt the entrances."

She took the black feather, pushing it into the pocket of her shorts. "It's probably a waste of time anyway."

"And why would that be?"

"Because I'm going to kill you myself if you don't stop calling me baby."

"Then don't anger me. Remember. You're mine." He pointed a finger at her. "Never forget."

"I know who belongs to who, Ibaelcaurzanon." Her victory was short lived when she found herself pressed against a wall, Remedy's hand around her throat.

His face was close to hers and flames leapt in his eyes. "You were told never to call me that."

Cassidy's hands reached for Remedy's but she stopped when she would have tugged at his grip. She raised her chin and met his gaze. "Go ahead. What are you waiting for?"

"Don't try my patience. One day I will kill you. Anger will eventually win out over self preservation."

Cassidy continued to stare at him, waiting. He

finally let go and stepped away. Her gaze never left his. She didn't know what she felt. Fear. Emptiness. Triumph. Or maybe some screwed up combination of all of them. "You don't call me baby and I won't call you by your true name."

Silence stretched out. Remedy nodded then turned to walk away, his wings tucked in close to his body.

"Wait." Cassidy pushed away from the wall.

Remedy faced her, his wings seeming to fade into him as he did. He still remained shirtless. "What do you want now?"

She ignored the irritation in his voice. "Why did you take me to the demon hunters last night?"

"To train you."

Cassidy shook her head. "No. Why last night? Why not earlier? And don't bother lying to me either."

Remedy inclined his head. "You have figured that out, have you? It works both ways. I can taste the lies on your lips too."

Cassidy tried to hide the shock she felt at his words. Taste the lies? How the hell was she meant to do that? And did it really matter if he already thought she could? "Well?"

"Our bond is now known by some. A human is much easier to destroy than a demon. We tend to survive nearly anything. They will come hunting. Don't do anything stupid." He turned again and walked away.

Cassidy watched him go, fear taking over once he was gone. She slid down the wall to sit on the floor. Hunting. Demons were hunting her? She closed her eyes and tilted her head back. So much for her father's promise that life would get better for them.

"Damn it." She banged her head against the wall, wincing at the pain. "I haven't got this far to curl up and die." She forced herself to her feet. She'd salt the entrances and then figure out how to become the hunter rather than the prey. There was no way she was going to spend her time cowering in her house. Not with eternity stretching out before her. She'd go crazy if she did. Picking up the grocery bags, she headed for the kitchen, turning the light on as she entered the room. Dropping the groceries on the floor, she stared at the swords and daggers scattered across the table. She guessed Remedy had come here before he'd tracked her down at the supermarket. Picking up one of the daggers, she slid it out of its sheath, eyeing the sharp blade.

Tomorrow night she was going hunting. Demons better look out because she wasn't about to tolerate any of them in her town. She thought of Remedy. Okay, but only one.

Chapter Nine

The next evening Cassidy kicked the stand down on her new motorbike and swung her leg over as she unbuckled her helmet to hang it on the handlebars. She glanced around, wishing she could see in the dark. She slid the two daggers out of their sheaths in her motorbike boots and closed her eyes. It didn't help. She couldn't hear anything unusual, but she could feel the demon. He had to be here somewhere. Her mark burned. Opening her eyes she sighed. Her first attempt at being a hunter wasn't going too well. She didn't have a clue what she should be doing. All those how-to videos hadn't prepared her for tracking down demons. Hopefully they'd taught her something about fighting.

She took a hesitant step forward then straightened her shoulders, forcing herself to stride into the shadows. She could feel him in her mark. Could feel the direction she needed to go. But she still couldn't see him. There was a rush of air and she raised an arm as she ducked, feeling an impact on her blade. She spun, trying to see better. Maybe she should have waited for a full moon. How could she attack what she couldn't see?

Laughter filled the air. "What are you? Demon or hunter?"

"Why don't you come and find out?" Her words sounded way braver than she felt. There was another rush of air and the shadows seemed to leap on her. She screamed as her hair was grabbed and she was forced to the ground.

The demon sniffed at her skin. "Either way, you smell delicious."

"Remedy!" Fear forced the name from her lips. There was no answer. She was going to die. It had all been for nothing. Months of nightmares, guilt, struggling to keep going and it was going to end here. Pressed against the ground and as helpless as a child.

"So delicious. Hot sweet blood. I can smell it through your skin." The demon ripped one of her daggers from her hand, throwing it away.

She couldn't move with her hair gripped tight against her scalp pressing her head into the ground, the demon's body holding hers down. Blood. What had Remedy said about blood? Blood brings us forth. She felt gravel under her left arm and ground her arm into it. "Remedy!" Screaming his name, she wondered if she should have used his true name. But he'd told her never to speak it out loud.

"Blood," the demon hissed before he pulled her left arm to him. Then he was gone and Cassidy was free. She struggled to her feet, still clutching one dagger. She spun around, trying to see what was happening, but she could only hear noises. The rush of air, the beat of wings, then a scream of terror.

"Mine. Do you hear me? Mine." Remedy's voice rang out over the whimper of the other demon.

Silence fell around Cassidy. She slowly turned around, trying to figure out where Remedy was. She froze as she felt movement behind her.

Remedy grabbed her hair, pulling her head back against him. "What were you thinking?" When she didn't answer he demanded, "Well? I should kill you now. Better to die by my own hand then that of a minor demon."

She struggled to get away from him, but he gripped her hair too tight. "Let me go," she said through clenched teeth.

"I sent you to demon hunters. Didn't you learn anything from them?"

"That I'm doomed for a sinner and dead by the first demon I meet."

Remedy pulled on her hair so she was forced to face him, his eyes a fiery gleam in the night. "Then use what you do have. What is the use of having my blood if you're not going to use it?"

No one told her anything. "How the hell am I meant to do that?"

He lifted her left arm. "Like you did. Blood. It binds, it empowers, it feeds. Blood is everything with demons." He brought her arm to his mouth, licking the blood from her torn flesh.

Pain arrowed through Cassidy and she gritted her teeth, unable to prevent an initial gasp. She pulled her arm away from him. "I'm not on the menu."

"It looked that way earlier." He released her and she staggered. "Go home."

She raised her chin. "Don't order me around."

"You're the one who called me."

"Would you rather I didn't?" Silence hung in the air and she wished she could see him clearly.

"Go home."

She felt him leave and her body began to tremble. She sheathed her dagger before she ended up cutting herself and walked unsteadily to her motorbike. The other dagger she gave up for lost. When she reached her motorbike she sagged against it, trying to steady her breathing. Maybe she should have stuck with a car. She forced herself to straighten. No. This was her choice. She'd had enough decisions taken from her hands. This one was hers.

Feeling steadier she pulled on her helmet and started the engine. When she reached home, she found her other dagger on the bedside table. A single droplet of blood rested on the blade. She stared at it. What was he trying to tell her? She spun when she felt him arrive.

"We are even." Remedy nodded towards the dagger.

Cassidy continued to stare at him.

"Have you changed your mind? Are we no longer partners?"

She felt like swearing and throwing something. Instead she remained still, meeting his gaze. She wished someone had written a manual on being bound to a demon. Information was a desperate need. Still holding his gaze, she reached for the dagger and lifted it. The flames in his eyes danced as she wiped the blood off with her finger and put it in her mouth.

She tensed at the sharp pain that hit her, refusing to break eye contact.

"Use the blood when you're in a fight. You could have beaten that demon effortlessly. My blood is far more powerful than his."

"How?"

Remedy lifted her left arm and took the dagger from her. He pressed the edge of the blade across the demon mark and slid it towards him. She hissed as a thin line of blood formed on her skin. "Close your eyes." When she obeyed, he ran his fingers across her skin, smearing the blood over her wrist. The demon mark writhed under her skin. His voice lowered. "Feel it? Feel my blood feeding? Feel it strengthening? This is our link. The demon mark. Use it, feed it. Catch hold of our bond and let its power fill you."

Cassidy felt it. Like a sluggish creature trying to slide away. She grabbed hold of it and forced it to obey. Energy flared through her and Remedy chuckled. She opened her eyes to stare at him. The flames in his eyes leapt high.

"Keep hold of that energy." He let go of her arm. "And don't let anyone past your guard."

The room seemed brighter than it ever had before. Her muscles bunched and she wanted to do something. Anything. Remedy swung at her and she reacted automatically, blocking and dodging. She grinned when he laughed, the power flowing through her making her feel invincible. Now she felt like a hunter. Demons better watch out.

"That is what you should have done earlier. Next time fight them with power. You are more than human. Don't forget it."

Cassidy watched as he strode across her bedroom to the window. "Remedy." He turned to face her. "I want the one who sent my father to you."

"You and me both." He met her gaze. "You're not ready. Not yet." He climbed out the window.

This time she saw him move away into the night. Her mouth dropped open as she stared after him. A few seconds later she was at her window, peering outside. The moon was no bigger than it had been earlier. She could see in the dark. Tomorrow night she'd hunt again. This time she knew how to do it. And she wasn't going to let a demon get the upper hand.

She grabbed a handful of hair, glaring at the long, reddish brown strands. It'd have to go. Tomorrow she'd visit a hairdresser and get it cut short. She rubbed the strands of hair between her fingers. She'd never had short hair before. Pushing her hair out of the way she reminded herself there was a lot of things she hadn't done before. But she wasn't about to let that stop her.

Her finger trailed along the cut Remedy had made on her wrist. The blood had started to congeal. She'd get used to new things. Her survival depended on it. An image of her father lying on the floor, the dagger in his chest, came to mind. This time she didn't push it immediately from her. The demon who'd sent him to Remedy would pay. Her gaze remained on her wrist. He'd pay in blood.

Chapter Ten

Cassidy groaned as her alarm clock turned on, the radio station interrupting her sleep. She rolled onto her back to stare at the ceiling. She smiled as she realised what song was playing. 'Boulevard of Broken Dreams'. She'd walked the streets alone every night this past week while everyone slept. Her only company had been demons. And they didn't stick around long. She had to find a way to get rid of them permanently, not fight them until they fled. Maybe she should ring the hunters and see what they knew. Surely there was some way to get rid of them. Some way that didn't involve joining their religion and following their strict rules. She didn't believe in their God. No, he'd failed her far too many times.

Her mum staring at her, asking her who she was came to mind, quickly followed by her father lying in a pool of his own blood. How could she worship someone who hadn't been there for her? If they couldn't tell her how to get rid of demons without being like them, then she'd figure it out on her own. Somehow.

The song ended and she turned off the alarm clock, rising to her feet. Tomorrow, before she went to sleep, she'd get in touch with the demon hunters. Ringing someone at eleven p.m. probably wasn't a good idea. She ran her fingers through her short hair. She'd considered getting a mohawk, but had decided that was probably too drastic for her first time with short hair. Instead she'd gone with a jagged, anime kind of look. A style that didn't need a mirror to look after it. Her mirrors were staying painted. There was no way she wanted to face her father's accusing eyes every day.

It didn't take her long to dress in black jeans and shirt, grab an apple to eat and put her daggers in her boots before she headed off on her motorbike. She was drawn towards the city centre, parking her bike in an area that was filled with the noise from nearby nightclubs.

Laughter and music wafted on the air. Cassidy ignored those in favour of tracking down the demon she felt nearby. She ran her fingernails along the scab she kept breaking open from the cut Remedy had made on her wrist. It was probably going to scar at this rate. Blood formed along the line and she smeared it across her demon mark. Energy flared, the night grew brighter and power flowed through her. Then she caught scent of it and raced through the streets, coming to a dead end. And there he was, a young woman passed out at his feet where he bent over her.

He reminded Cassidy of a spider, long joints, narrow limbs, fangs and grey skin that seemed stretched to a translucent thinness. She pulled her daggers from her boots, her lips curving into a mirthless smile. "Why don't you pick on someone your own size?"

The demon leapt at her. She struck out at him, jumping to the side, barely avoiding his blade like claws. He stalked around her and she slowly turned, keeping him in view. He threw himself at her again, screeching when he missed her. But she didn't. Her blade slid along his flesh and dark liquid spilled over the grey of his skin. He howled and launched himself at her again.

"Is that the best you can do?" She couldn't resist taunting him. "It sucks when your prey fights back, doesn't it?" She spared a quick glance for the body lying on the ground, unmoving. She hoped she hadn't been too late to save the woman.

"Prey." The demon spat the word out. "Prey is human. You are more demon than me." He leapt at the nearby building and, digging claws into the wall, scurried up the side.

Cassidy swore as she watched him flee, then spun when she heard a noise behind her. "Gabe." She said his name like it was a swear word.

He grinned at her. "Hello, bad influence. Nice to see you missed me. I like what you've done with your hair."

She ignored the compliment. "How'd you find me?"

"Do you really need to ask, demon girl?" He gestured towards her wrist. "You might as well have taken out a billboard sign saying demon tainted here. I'm surprised a heap of demons haven't headed this way to check out what's going on."

"What are you doing here?" She looked behind him. "Alone. Without your babysitter."

Gabe's grin faded. "He's a year younger than me. Besides I'm too old to need a babysitter."

"How old are you?"

"Twenty-one."

"You never said why you're here."

"You seemed more concerned about my cousin's location than wanting an answer." He held up a hand when she glared at him. "All right. No need to get upset. I don't spend all my time hunting demons. I was at a nightclub."

"A nightclub." She knew she sounded sceptical, but that didn't sound like something a hunter did. Not from what she'd read in Patrick's book.

"I'd offer to buy you a drink but they're afraid I'll escape if they give me more than a few dollars at a time."

"Escape from what?"

"Escape to."

"Escape to what, then."

"To bad influences." He grinned, taking a step towards her. "But it looks like one found me instead. So bad influence, what happened to your pet demon?"

Cassidy shrugged as she returned her daggers to her boots. It felt odd holding onto them when she wasn't fighting. "Don't know and don't care." She looked around, flaring the demon blood as she did. She felt a tug in one direction. There were still more demons in her city. "I was going to ring one of you in the morning."

"What for?"

"I want to get rid of demons, not let them escape. How can I do that?"

"You can never get rid of them permanently, just send them to hell. But they're stuck there until they're called by name or they're first to answer the call of a human looking for any demon."

"Is this going to be one of those conversations that take forever? I've got things to do." She looked back in the direction she needed to head in next. She'd have to get her motorbike first. The demon wasn't within walking distance.

"Like what?" Gabe stepped past her with a frown. "Is that a body?"

Cassidy swore. "I forgot about her." She spun and hurried to the still limp body to stand and stare down at her. She couldn't bring herself to check the pulse. What if she was dead? An image of her father, knife in his chest, flashed through her mind.

Gabe reached her side and crouched beside the woman, his fingers going to her neck. "She's alive." He rose to his feet. "Come on. The sooner we get away from here the sooner we can get someone to rescue her."

"We're just going to leave her here?"

Gabe reached for her hand and tugged her forward. "The last thing we want is to be in every second police report. Things like that start to ring alarm bells."

Cassidy allowed him to lead her away from the area. He dropped her hand once they reached a street sign and pulled his phone out to send a text message. "Who'd you let know?"

"Family. They'll make sure the message gets to the appropriate person. So, where to next?"

"You're not going anywhere with me. I hunt alone." She pressed a hand against his chest when he tried to come closer.

"Alone, huh? Fine. I'll stand in the shadows and watch."

"You weren't invited."

Gabe grinned. "If I waited for you to invite me I'd go grey." He looked around. "So where is it?"

Cassidy shook her head, striding in the direction of her motorbike. She glared at Gabe when he fell into step with her. "Don't you understand the word no?"

"Nope." His grin faded. "I want to see how you hunt. You're so far from sainthood it should be impossible. At least from what I know."

She reached her motorbike and turned to look at him. "And why's that any of your business?"

"Because I love to hunt demons. It's the rest of it I have trouble with."

"The rest of what?"

Gabe's lips twisted into a smile. "Let's just say I'd never attain sainthood."

"Bad influences?"

Gabe laughed. "I think the problem is that I'm the bad influence." He sobered. "This is meant to be my last chance to be a hunter. I don't think I'm going to pass the exam."

Cassidy's eyes narrowed. "I thought there was no exam."

"Not officially. But you might as well say we're being tested all the time. If they handed out grades I don't think they'd be able to find one low enough for me."

Cassidy picked up her helmet. "I haven't got a spare one."

Gabe shrugged. "So don't stack it and I won't miss having one."

She studied his face. His gaze was so intense she wondered if he could see in the dark as clearly as she could. She nodded and swung her leg over the motorbike. "Get on then." She waited until he was behind her, his hands lightly resting on her hips, his legs alongside hers.

"Thanks."

"Don't thank me yet. We haven't reached our destination."

Gabe laughed. "Then what are we waiting for?"

Cassidy took off faster than she normally would and grinned as he tightened his grip. It took nearly a quarter of an hour before they were close to the next demon. She parked her motorbike and they both hopped off. Spotting the demon ahead of them, strolling along the road, she drew her daggers.

Gabe put a hand on her arm. "No. It hasn't done anything yet."

"It's a demon."

Gabe sighed. "Until we have proof a demon means harm we can't act against it."

Energy flared through her as she spun to face Gabe. "What sort of rubbish is that?"

Chapter Eleven

Gabe didn't get a chance to reply. At the flare of demon energy, the demon's wings snapped out and he flew at them, claws extended. Gabe laughed as Cassidy blocked, spinning away from him to put space between them. "Now we have proof."

"About bloody time," Cassidy muttered. She warily watched the demon who hovered just out of reach. "Come down here and fight me."

"What are you?" the demon demanded.

Gabe gestured towards the weapons she held. "Think I can have one of them daggers?"

Ignoring the demon's question, Cassidy threw one towards him. "What do we do now?"

Gabe caught the dagger and tipped some of the contents from a vial of liquid over it. He capped the vial and called out, "Here." When Cassidy nodded he threw the vial. "Tip some of that onto your blade."

She did as he suggested. "What is it?"

"Holy water. They love fire and could bath in it. This feels to them what fire feels to us."

"Great, now we've just got to get the creature to come closer." Which looked like it might be a problem since the demon was rising higher into the air.

"No we don't." Gabe grinned and turned the dagger so he held it by the blade. "Get ready." He tossed the dagger at the demon who howled as he plummeted to the ground.

Cassidy was on him in an instant, sinking her blade into his body. The creature howled again, striking out at her. She dodged and weaved, striking back. Then Gabe was beside her, having collected the dagger. He plunged the weapon into the demon and started to pray. Falling backwards, Cassidy swore at the pain Gabe's words caused. Jumping to her feet, she struck out at him with her forearm. "Shut up you idiot."

Gabe grinned up at her as he fought to keep the demon pinned to the ground. "What's up, demon girl?"

She gestured at him with her middle finger before she launched herself on the demon again. The creature howled and fought, struggling to escape. Its skin smoked and Cassidy stabbed it again at the same moment Gabe did. The demon seemed to shrink in on itself, becoming nothing.

Rising to her feet, Cassidy barely had time to sheath her dagger before Gabe whooped and grabbed hold of her to whirl her around. When his lips came close to hers, she turned her head and pressed against his chest, pulling away from him. "No, don't. Remedy will kill you."

Gabe let her go. "You're… dating him?" He sounded horrified.

"No!" She shouted the word then forced herself to calm down. "No. Never." Date one of her father's killers? Was he crazy?

"Then what?"

"He thinks he owns me." She turned her back on Gabe and felt his hand rest on her shoulder. "It'd be safer if you left me alone."

"Cassidy–"

There was a rush of air and Remedy forced himself between the two of them, his hand going around Gabe's throat. "Don't touch what's not yours."

Cassidy threw herself at Remedy, fear for Gabe rushing through her. "Leave him alone." She pulled at Remedy's hand, trying to help Gabe who was struggling to escape. "Damn you. Let him go, now."

Remedy opened his hand and Gabe dropped to the ground where he staggered to his feet, rubbing at his neck. Remedy turned his burning gaze on Cassidy. "You were warned. I said I'd kill any who touched you."

"We were celebrating getting rid of a demon. It was nothing more." She yelled the words at Remedy, fear still racing through her. "Stop screwing up my life."

"You are mine." He pointed a finger at her. "Never forget it."

"I belong to no one." Her face was so close to Remedy's she could see the individual flames in his eyes as she yelled at him. "Got it? No one."

"I say different."

"What would make you let her go?" Gabe asked.

Remedy and Cassidy both turned to look at him. Cassidy spoke first. "I'm bound to him."

"Only death would break the binding," Remedy said. "It would kill both of us. And I don't plan to die."

Gabe shook his head. "No. What would she have to do before you'd let her live her life? What favour do you need done?"

"My enemy made powerless against me."

Cassidy's anger faded and she stared at Remedy, hope struggling to form. "Your enemy."

Remedy nodded. "The one who sent your father to me."

Hope and anger rose together within her, hatred sprinkled amongst it. "Done. Now who is he?"

"Do you think you have the ability to make him powerless? He has ultimate power over me. How can you solve that problem?"

Cassidy shrugged. "I don't know, but I'm going to find out."

"He knows your name?" Gabe asked Remedy.

Remedy sneered at Gabe, refusing to answer his question.

"Yeah, he does," Cassidy said.

Gabe slowly shook his head. "You're screwed then."

"No. It's just going to take some time to figure this one out."

Gabe stopped shaking his head. "Maybe not." He stared silently at her for a moment. "Demon girl, it just might be your lucky day to be a sinner."

"Forget the theatrics and spit it out."

"You could bind him to an object."

"No she couldn't," Remedy said. "He's too powerful."

"He'll be imprisoned in the object?" Cassidy asked.

Gabe ignored Cassidy's question to meet Remedy's eyes. "How powerful is he?"

"As powerful as me."

"I want to try," Cassidy said.

"No," Gabe and Remedy answered in unison.

Cassidy glared at them, refusing to believe she couldn't do it. Instead of arguing she shrugged her shoulders. She wasn't about to waste her time in an argument she didn't need. Somehow she'd figure it out, with or without their help. She turned her gaze on Gabe. "Do you want a lift home?"

Gabe's eyes narrowed, their intensity increasing. Then he chuckled. "You're still going to do it, aren't you?"

"I will not allow it," Remedy said.

Cassidy's hands went to her hips. "Do you want a lift home or not?"

With a nod Gabe handed the dagger back to her. "It'd be easier than hitchhiking." He grinned. "Not sure if it'd be safer though." He shot a glance at Remedy.

Remedy pointed a finger at him. "Just remember she's mine."

Gabe met his stare, saying nothing, then turned to Cassidy. "Think you can remember how to get there?"

Cassidy nodded before she strode to her motorbike, swinging her leg over the seat as she donned her helmet. She waited for Gabe to hop on the back, smiling when his arms wrapped tightly around her middle. She wondered if it was for Remedy's benefit or because of the way she rode. She took off, hoping it was for Remedy. That demon did not own her.

When they pulled up out the front of Gabe's home, dawn was starting to streak the horizon with colour. She was tired, but energy still coursed through her making her wish there were more demons to hunt.

"Thanks for the lift." Gabe stood beside her. He grinned. "And the hunt."

Cassidy nodded, removing her helmet. "It was different fighting with someone else. And I want holy water. Hundreds of litres of it."

Gabe laughed. "Blood thirsty, aren't you?"

"And you're not?"

Gabe's grin faded. "I've never had a problem with the hunting part. It's the not sinning I have an issue with." He took a step closer and lowered his voice. "Temptation's always been my weakness."

Cassidy met his gaze and her mouth dried at his expression. She reached for him then pulled her hand back before she could touch. She shook her head. "Don't. He'll kill you."

Gabe's lips curved slightly. "Temptation and danger. My greatest weaknesses."

"Then I won't be very interesting once I deal with Remedy's enemy."

"Oh you'll always be dangerous, demon girl." Gabe grinned. "Wanna hunt tonight? I'll bring my own weapons this time and enough holy water for both of us."

She remembered the satisfaction it had given her to vanquish the demon. Hunting alone might be her preference, but she'd actually managed to get rid of a demon with Gabe's help. "Deal." She pulled her helmet back on and headed for home, still smiling.

Chapter Twelve

Cassidy glared at her home phone when it rang out again. Where was Gabe? She'd rung him at least four times already today. She'd waited until lunchtime to give him time to sleep. Where the hell was he? Or was he ignoring her calls? He'd been the one to offer his help. So why wasn't he answering the phone? She slammed the cordless phone back in its cradle when it rang out again.

She spent the rest of the afternoon pacing the house, too restless to do anything else. When Gabe finally returned her calls, she demanded, "Where've you been?"

"Sleeping. Not all of us run on demon energy."

"I need to know more about binding a demon."

"Look, I shouldn't have said anything about it to you. My cousin wants to come and talk to you."

"Riley?"

"No. Scarlett. Well, she's actually my second or third cousin. Possibly even my fourth. It gets confusing. Anyway, you haven't met her. Can I bring her over? And where do you live?"

"Does she know how to do it?"

"More than she wishes sometimes."

"Then I want to talk to her." Cassidy rattled off her address then had to wait until Gabe found pen and paper to write it down.

"We'll be there in about an hour."

The next hour passed far too slowly for Cassidy. She continued to pace through the house, occasionally stopping to look at an object and remember better days. And to think she'd thought nothing could get worse than her mum having early onset Alzheimer's. But how could she have even considered demons existed? No one believed in them. Or if they did, it was usually because they were crazy. Isn't that what she'd thought of her father? How many other people who were considered crazy for believing in demons were actually sane?

When she heard the knock at her front door, she raced through the house to throw the door open. Three people stood on her doorstep.

Gabe grinned at her and pointed to his companions in turn. "Jesse. Scarlett."

Jesse had eyes dark enough to be black, an angular face with slashing cheeks, close cropped dark hair, broad shoulders, a row of earrings up both ears and in one eyebrow. Scarlett wore a small gold cross on a cord necklace around her throat, had warm brown eyes, a wiry frame and short blond hair that feathered around her fine boned face. The three of them were dressed in black jeans and short sleeved shirts and had demon marks around their left wrists.

Cassidy stepped back so they could enter and led them to her lounge room. She waited until they were seated before she spoke to Scarlett. "Gabe said you know about binding demons."

"You should be trying to get rid of the demon currently bound to you instead of collecting more," Scarlett said.

"No way. I wouldn't survive a minute against demons without him."

"You wouldn't have to fight alone. No one should take on a demon alone," Scarlett said.

"I prefer to fight alone. You can't rely on people. Ever. This," she touched her mark that moved slightly under her skin, "Is what allows me to kick demon butt. In fact, I could probably take on all of you and win."

Jesse grinned, slightly predatory. "I wouldn't count on that, demon girl."

Heat flared in Cassidy's mark and she was out of the seat in a second and across the room to grab one of the many daggers she'd stashed around her house. "What are you?" Her eyes narrowed as she stared at Jesse, the dagger unsheathed and pointed towards him.

All the demon hunters were on their feet, but before Jesse could reply, Scarlett stepped forward, a hand gesture holding her companions back. "We're not here to hurt you, Cassidy."

"Then what is he? And how could he get past the salt across my front doorstep?"

"He used to be a demon, but he's human now."

Cassidy shook her head at Scarlett's words. "That wasn't human I felt."

"There's a slight trace of demon still left in him. But he won't hurt you. None of us are here to hurt you. We want to help you get rid of Remedy." Scarlett took a step forward. "I'm sure we can figure this out." Another step forward.

Cassidy still held her dagger protectively in front of her. "All I want to know is how to bind a demon. I'm keeping Remedy. I read Demonology. That's not me. I don't believe in all that religious crap."

"How can you not believe? All these demons, don't they prove anything to you?" Scarlett asked.

"Yeah, that humans aren't top of the food chain like they believe. And those bastards better watch out when I'm around. I'm nobody's prey."

Scarlett winced at her choice of words.

Gabe grinned. "Didn't I tell you she was extremely likeable?"

Scarlett sent Gabe a pointed look. "No wonder your mum was concerned for your soul, Gabriel."

Gabe shrugged. "If she didn't have me to worry over she'd find something else. I'm doing her a favour."

Scarlett slowly shook her head at him before she turned back to Cassidy. "You don't understand how dangerous it is to bind a demon to an object. You won't live forever. Anyone could end up with it. A demon in the wrong hands can do a lot of damage."

"That's not going to be a problem."

Scarlett frowned. "Dying?"

Cassidy nodded.

Jesse swore, ignoring Scarlett's rebuke over his language. "No wonder Gabe calls you demon girl. Have you any idea what you've done?"

"No. And I wish people would stop asking me that." Cassidy lowered her dagger, but continued to hold it. "No one will tell me anything. Well, not anything I want to hear. I'm not religious and not interested." Not after everything she'd been through. "So don't bother trying to force it down my throat. I'm keeping Remedy. That's not up for discussion. All I need to know is how to get rid of our enemy."

"Who happens to know his true name," Gabe reminded her.

Cassidy shrugged. "Yeah, and?"

Jesse shook his head. "You're screwed."

"Jesse!" Scarlett glared at him.

It was Jesse's turn to shrug, a half smile on his lips. "You know it as well as I do, Lady Knight."

"I wouldn't have worded it quite that way," Scarlett said.

Jesse's half smile became a grin. "It doesn't matter how it's worded, the fact remains. She's got no hope in hell in retaining a grip on her humanity. A demon that powerful will eventually take her over."

Cassidy stared at him, wanting to demand he take back his words. Remedy wasn't going to own her. He'd already taken enough from her. "How do I stop that?"

"Sever the ties somehow," Jesse said.

"Or become more powerful than him." Gabe's soft words caused bedlam.

Cassidy watched as an argument broke out amongst the hunters about the morality of binding a demon to an object. When it looked like it wasn't going to end, she broke in. "What's the best object to use?"

"Don't even think about it," Scarlett said.

At the same time Gabe answered her. "A ring."

"Why a ring?" Ignoring Scarlett, Cassidy turned to Gabe.

"Jewellery is best since you can always have it on you. A bracelet or necklace risk being broken in battle. The only way you'll lose a ring is if your finger is cut off or you lose weight."

Cassidy shuddered at the thought of her finger being cut off. "So I get one that's tight on me now and avoid axe wielding maniacs."

Gabe laughed. "Want help choosing one?"

"No." Scarlett grabbed his shoulder, turning him to face her. "Stop encouraging her, Gabriel. Your mother didn't leave you with us so you could get into more trouble."

Gabe's eyes narrowed. "Stop calling me that. Only Mum calls me that stupid name. I'm not an angel and I've got no interest in becoming one. And stop treating me like a child. I'm an adult, Scarlett. Quite capable of making my own choices."

"Really? Then think about what you're doing. You help her and you imperil your own soul," Scarlett said.

"Like you did?"

Scarlett looked away from Gabe's intense stare. "Sometimes one must choose the lesser evil." She looked at Cassidy. "But this isn't the case here. We can solve this problem without sin. We'll find a way."

"You're already too late. My sins can't get much worse than they already are." Cassidy's lips twisted into a mocking smile as she remembered the night she'd first met Remedy. "You can't save me from hell. You're a few months too late."

Scarlet walked towards Cassidy, compassion filling her gaze. "All sins can be forgiven. You only have to be sorry, never do it again and ask forgiveness. All sinners can repent."

Cassidy laughed, short and sharp. "This one is impossible to repeat, except in my nightmares." She made a sharp motion with her hand. "Forget it. I can't follow your way. I have my own way of doing things. Now are you going to help me or not?"

Scarlet shook her head. "I can't. I'm sorry. Not again. If you're willing to try other paths then I'll help, but this," she glanced towards Jesse before meeting Cassidy's gaze, "Is a sin. One I can't repeat. Not and live with my actions."

Jesse stepped close to Scarlett, draping an arm around her to pull her against him. "If you want help getting rid of the demon call us. In the meantime," he pulled a vial from his pocket and tossed it to her. She noticed a black feather tattooed on his left palm. "You might want to think about why holy water would hurt a human."

Cassidy stared at the vial in her hands. "What?"

"Spill a few drops on yourself. Maybe on that cut across your mark. And try praying," Jesse said.

"I don't know what you're trying to prove." Cassidy slid the vial into a pocket. It would come in handy when she hunted later. On her weapons, not herself. "There's nothing wrong with me."

Jesse smiled slightly. "I never claimed there was. I just want you to think about what it means." His smile widened. "I have nothing against demons. They're a little like humans. Some choose to practice evil, some choose more innocuous pursuits."

"And what about you? What was your sin when you were a demon?" Cassidy asked.

Jesse laughed. "Lust."

"That's not a sin," Cassidy protested.

It was Gabe's turn to laugh. "And you wonder why I have issues with being a hunter."

Cassidy's eyes rounded. "You can't have sex if you're a hunter?"

"Of course you can," Scarlett said.

"As long as you're married," Jesse explained.

"And wanting to sleep with someone isn't a good enough reason to get married," Gabe said.

Cassidy shook her head. "You lot live in the dark ages."

"Yeah. Is it any wonder I want to escape?"

Scarlett's gaze turned to Gabe. "No one is holding you prisoner. No one is making you be a hunter."

"It's not hunting I have an issue with. In fact, that's the only thing I don't have an issue with." Gabe turned his intense stare to Cassidy. "Want help finding a ring?"

"Gabriel-" Scarlett broke off at the glare he sent her way.

"Yeah," Cassidy said before another argument could break out.

Gabe nodded at Cassidy before he turned back to Scarlett. "I'll find my own way home."

"I hope you can." Scarlett pulled away from Jesse and wrapped her arms around Gabe. "Take care,

Gabriel. You're family. No matter the path you take we'll pray for you."

Gabe's arms tightened around her before he stepped away. "Thanks, little cousin." He grinned. "Maybe you should have Father Joe make a vat of holy water." He glanced towards Cassidy. "I reckon we're going to need it."

"There's more holy water at Gran's," Scarlet said.

"Here." Jesse tossed a vial to Gabe.

"How many of them do you have?" Cassidy asked.

"One left." Jesse shrugged with a grin. "I like to be prepared." He turned to Scarlett. "Ready to go home?"

Chapter Thirteen

Scarlet stared at him a moment before she nodded then turned to Cassidy. "Be careful and call us if you need help." When Cassidy opened her mouth to speak Scarlett held up a hand. "Help we can give." Her gaze darted to Gabe then back to Cassidy. "Gabriel has my number if you need it."

Cassidy nodded and walked to the front door with Scarlett and Jesse. When she returned to the lounge room, she found Gabe draped over one of the armchairs, tossing a dagger into the air and catching it.

"Is that one of mine?"

Gabe caught the dagger and turned to her with a grin. "How many have you got hidden around this place?"

She shrugged. "A few." At his raised brow she shrugged again. "Maybe a bit more than a few."

"Paranoid much?" He swung his feet to the ground and stood up.

"Why were you checking out my place anyway?"

Gabe chuckled. "Paranoia."

Cassidy turned away before she let a grin escape. She returned the dagger she held to its hiding place. "Put that back where you found it."

Gabe returned the dagger to the small space between the floor and the armchair he'd been using. "Anyone else live here with you?"

"No."

"Why not?"

"Because there's no one." The image of her father lying in a pool of his own blood came to mind.

"Got a spare room?"

Cassidy stared at him, hands on her hips. "You did not just invite yourself to move in, did you?"

Gabe chuckled. "Yep. So what do you say? I'm a good cook."

"And what about the dishes? Do you do them?" When Gabe strode across the room towards her, Cassidy forced herself to stay still, fighting the urge to take a step backwards. She regularly found his gaze unnerving. It felt like he could see inside her to all the secrets she wanted to keep hidden. Every single blood soaked sin.

"It's not like I'm asking to marry you. I'm looking for a bed for a few weeks until I can get a job that'll fit in with hunting." He grimaced. "There aren't that many of them. I'll cook the meals and whatever else needs doing. My family will give me food, but they won't give me money. It might not sound like much of a bargain, but I will hunt with you."

She was beginning to rethink his offer. She hadn't known he'd want to move in with her. "I hunt alone."

"Really? What about last night?"

"You have a bad habit of inviting yourself along, don't you?"

Gabe chuckled. "You're not the first person who's tried to tell me I'm pushy. So what do you say? I'll get you more of this." A vial of holy water appeared in his hand.

Cassidy stared at it. "You won't push your bible crap on me?"

His voice lowered. "Religion is the last thing I want to share with you."

Cassidy's gaze met his and held. Her lips parted and she tried to think of something to say. Anything. Then heat flared through her mark and she spun to see Remedy enter the lounge room.

"How many times do I need to tell you she's mine?"

Remedy stepped up to Gabe who met his gaze without flinching.

"Does Cassidy feel the same way?"

"Do you think I care how she feels? She chose this. Her words, her actions made her mine. Now she must live with her choice." He jabbed a finger at Gabe's chest. "You leave her alone."

"We were just about to go out looking for a ring." Gabe's lips slowly curved into a smile. Remedy roared, swinging at Gabe who ducked and spun, coming up to the side of him.

Cassidy yelled at them, throwing herself between them. "Enough. Are you freaking crazy?" She stared at Gabe, her arms around Remedy who vibrated with energy. "You want to move in with me and yet you keep baiting my demon. Are you suicidal?"

"If that's my two choices I'll go with crazy."

"Stop calling me your demon like I'm some possession," Remedy growled.

Cassidy looked up at Remedy. "You back off. I've got this under control. Or I did before you arrived. And how the hell did it get to sunset already?" She pushed Remedy away from her, making sure the direction was also away from Gabe too. She sighed and pointed a warning finger at Gabe. "No more baiting or you can sleep in the gutter for all I care.

You can't kill him, not without killing me." She turned back to Remedy. "And I need to buy a ring to bind our enemy."

"No. You're not to throw your life away on a useless task." Remedy's voice boomed through the room.

Cassidy winced, barely stopping herself from covering her ears with her hands. "What am I meant to do? Wait for him to kill you? Us?"

Remedy shook his head. "I have kept one step ahead of him for centuries. I can continue to do so. You'll have to leave here. I'll find somewhere safer for you to hide."

"No. This is my home. I've spent my entire life here. No one's chasing me from my own home." Cassidy's hands went to her hips and she glared at Remedy. Hadn't he taken enough from her already?

"Have they told you how a demon is bound to an object?" When Cassidy shook her head, Remedy continued. "You need to mingle your blood and press that object between the two of you where the skin is broken. The hand is the part usually chosen. It's easier to clasp hands than anything else."

Cassidy's mouth dried and her heart felt like it paused. "How long?"

"As long as it takes to say the ritual."

"How long?" She stepped closer to Remedy. "Tell me how long."

"It would be like holding a dozen tigers for endless minutes. Do you think you can manage that?" Remedy's gaze flickered with flames that leapt higher when Gabe stepped forward.

He put a hand on Cassidy's shoulder and met Remedy's glare. "She has help."

"Why? What's in it for you, boy?"

"A lot of things."

"She'll never be yours, no matter the outcome," Remedy warned.

"If we do this she gains free choice. You don't own her or force her to do anything against her will."

"Neither of you will gain power over me. My name will not be used against me." Flames almost filled Remedy's gaze. "Or that will be the end of all of us. I will be no one's slave."

Cassidy suddenly realised what Remedy meant by being able to taste the truth of her words. She had never believed a statement more in her life. She licked her lips, swallowing past the lump that formed in her throat. "Equals. Partners."

Remedy's gaze dropped from Gabe's to hers. He held her gaze momentarily before he gave a sharp nod. His lips curved into a smile that would give nightmares. His teeth became sharp points under her gaze. He pressed them against his lip and broke the skin. "Sealed." His head lowered to hers.

Cassidy had no chance to step away before his lips were on hers, a sharp sting as the skin of her lip was broken, followed by the flare of pain as their blood mingled. She felt Remedy's hand at the back of her head, but still she tried to pull away. Then he released her and she staggered backwards.

Remedy turned his gaze on Gabe, his teeth even again, the smile remaining pure evil. "She's still mine. Don't forget that, boy." When Gabe nodded, Remedy strode from the room.

Cassidy's eyes closed when Remedy was gone and she swayed in place. When an arm encircled her waist her eyes flew open and she met Gabe's intense green stare. "Don't-" she pressed a hand against his chest.

"Shh. Sit down." He guided her to the lounge suite and sat beside her. "You okay?"

Cassidy stared at him a moment before she nodded. "Yeah. I think so."

Gabe grinned. "Not your boyfriend, huh? If you have a habit of randomly giving away kisses what happened to mine?"

Cassidy shoved Gabe away with a glare. "I didn't kiss him."

Gabe continued to grin at her from where he'd landed back against the cushions of the lounge suite. "I know. But at least now you don't look like you're going to pass out. Anger's better than running and hiding."

Cassidy took an unsteady breath. "Didn't you say something about taking me shopping for a ring?"

He rose smoothly to his feet, holding out a hand to her. "That's my girl. Come on then."

"Don't call me that."

He continued to hold out his hand. "Cassidy?"

"I prefer Cass." She took his hand and let him pull her to her feet. He was close enough she could feel the heat of his skin.

"Cass." The word was soft as his lips curved into a smile. "Want to go clubbing with me the night after we bind the demon?"

Cassidy stared at him a moment, then laughed. "Sure, why not." She pushed at his chest to make him step away from her. "Now about that ring."

"In a minute." He reached out and ran a finger across her bottom lip. "Blood." He wiped his finger on his jeans. "Now we can go."

Cassidy stared at him, wondering what Remedy would do if she gave into her current impulse. She blinked and looked away from Gabe. Remedy would probably kill Gabe before she could even think about stopping him. "I've got a spare helmet in the garage." When he nodded, she grabbed it and headed for the front door where her boots were kept. Once there'd been three pairs of shoes lined up by the door. One of them had been rainbow sneakers. They hadn't been rainbow coloured after she'd met Remedy. First they'd been red, then a rusty brown. They'd been burned along with the rest of her clothes. She stared at her boots.

"You okay?"

Giving Gabe the helmet, she pulled on her boots. She didn't have an answer for him. She didn't even have one for herself.

Chapter Fourteen

Cassidy stared at the case of rings in front of her. None of them seemed right. She was going to be stuck with the ring for a very long time. Forever. How could she pick one she'd always want to wear? It wasn't like she could swap it if she grew bored with it. She shook her head, turning to Gabe.

"None? Not even one?"

She heard the begging undertone in his voice, but ignored it to shake her head. She didn't blame him since she'd dragged him to five jewellery shops already. "No. There's nothing wrong with them, but they're just not…" she shrugged.

"The right one?" Gabe asked.

The assistant slid the case of rings back into the glass cabinet. "I don't know if this will help, but we have some estate rings out the back." He looked her up and down. "They might be a little out of your budget though."

"Cass?" Gabe prompted when she continued to stand there staring at the rings in the cabinet, rubbing her wrist.

She met his gaze. "We have other things we should be doing." She glanced at his mark.

Gabe nodded. "I know. But this is important too." He turned to the assistant. "Bring them out. No harm in looking." He grinned. "If I'm lucky she might even find one and stop dragging me to every shop in a hundred kilometre radius."

Cassidy lightly hit his arm with the back of her hand, glaring at him. "Liar."

"One moment," the assistant said before he stepped out the back.

Cassidy rubbed her wrist again, annoyed with the heat that continued to build. She looked up at Gabe, taking a step closer to him and dropping her voice. "What is out there?"

"I think the question is probably going to be how many are out there."

Cassidy's eyes widened as she stared up at him. "What are we going to do? And why don't they come in here?"

"They like to keep a low profile. Less hunters that way."

"Here we go." The assistant placed a case of rings on the counter between them.

Cassidy forced herself to pay attention and was glad she did. She reached out to lift a simple gold band that had open work vines twisted together between a narrow, solid border. The width of the ring was a centimetre and when she slid it on her finger it fit perfectly.

"Looks like we have a winner." Gabe grinned. "Finally."

Cassidy nodded and pulled out her EFTPOS card to pay for the ring. When she heard the price she was relieved her weekly income was so large. Then she instantly wished it wasn't.

Gabe linked his arm through hers as they left the shop. "That's not going to run you short is it?"

Cassidy shook her head. "I wish."

Gabe stared at her a moment as they continued to walk towards the shopping centre exit. "You say the oddest things sometimes."

Cassidy's jaw tightened. There was no way she could tell him about her father. If he'd still been alive she wouldn't have been able to afford the ring. If he'd still been alive, she wouldn't have needed to buy it.

She forced the thoughts from her mind. There were other things to deal with. "What are we going to do about our welcoming committee?"

"You could always call your boyfriend."

She sent him a pointed glance, ignoring the comment. "How do we figure out how many there are?"

"We don't. We get on your bike and get the hell out of Dodge."

"And what? Leave them here?"

Gabe shook his head. "Lead them somewhere else." He mentioned an old graveyard. "Do you know where it is?"

"Yeah."

"Then that's where we head. And pray to God we get there before them and you can enter hallowed ground."

She didn't bother pointing out to him that she couldn't pray. "Your plan has a lot of maybes." Cassidy came to a stop at the exit and stared through the open doors at the car park, stepping to one side as other shoppers came towards her. Heat from the night air wafted over her and she swore. "We're screwed."

"I don't suppose you have a spare key for your bike."

Cassidy nodded, unable to take her gaze from the demons scattered throughout the car park. She'd worried about what would happen if she'd ever lost her key during a fight. "It's taped between the seat and fuel tank." She couldn't stop looking at all the demons. Some of them looked human, but others looked very much like demons. "Why can't people see them? They should be running, screaming."

"Demons can hide themselves. It takes effort and it's usually easier for them to look human. Well, it is for those that have that ability. Some can't hide or look human. But obviously those ones aren't out there."

"Why?"

Gabe laughed. "Because people would be running, screaming."

"You're so annoying sometimes." She shot him another glare, her gaze instantly drawn back to the demons.

"Does that mean you're not going clubbing with me?"

"Focus, Gabriel." She grinned when his own faded at the use of his full name. "What are we going to do other than serve ourselves up on a platter with apples in our mouths?"

"The apples would be a waste of time, they wouldn't appreciate the effort."

"Gabriel." She ground his name out through clenched teeth.

"You head to the right, I'll go left. First to the bike picks up the other and then we get the hell out of here."

"Do you have a license?"

Gabe shook his head with a grin. "I think that's the least of our problems."

"A pity. It would have been nice if at least one of us had a license." She smiled at his expression. "Can you ride?"

"Like Evil Knievel."

"Isn't he a stunt rider?"

Gabe laughed.

"There's no way in hell you're getting to my bike first." She picked at the scab on her wrist and smeared the blood across her demon mark. She breathed deep as the energy rushed through her. "I'll pick you up soon." Then she was off, dashing through people, avoiding cars. She skidded to a stop at her bike, pulled on her helmet as she threw her leg over and started the engine, her helmet straps undone.

Gabe grabbed the spare helmet as he reached her

side, pulling it on as he mounted behind her. "Go. Now." When she took off, he yelled. "Faster."

"The cops-"

"Forget the bloody cops. Your boyfriend can deal with them."

"You call him my boyfriend one more time and I'm going to punch you." She accelerated rapidly, dodging traffic, heart racing as her gaze darted everywhere.

They reached the graveyard in record time and Cassidy ran towards the gates, Gabe on her heels. She tried to cross, but felt like she was slammed backwards as Gabe sprinted past her. She gasped in pain and stared at Gabe who turned to face her.

He swore, pulling a handful of fine, finger length blades from behind him. "Guess you're too demon for here."

"Where'd they come from?" Cassidy nodded towards the blades then glanced towards the horde of demons headed their way.

Gabe lifted a corner of his shirt to show a narrow leather band with more blades sticking up out of the pockets that ran the length of it. A few of them were a little larger and wider. "I told you I'd bring my own this time."

She held out a hand for one and weighted the slim blade in her hand. "How do you use them?"

"Throw them." He took it back with a glance towards the demons. "You sure you don't want to call your boyfriend?" He threw one of his blades as he stepped back into the sanctuary offered by the graveyard.

Cassidy didn't have time to answer. Drawing a dagger from her boot, she attacked the demon that launched itself at her. The night became a blur of attack, parry, blood and movement. She drew on all the demon energy she could, determined not to call Remedy. She could do this. She needed to do this. Then thought was impossible. Only action and reaction.

Swing, parry, block, dodge. It was like a dance. One that left her cut in several places. Each time she brushed her wrist over the blood and attacked harder with every new burst of energy. She was surrounded, attacking in all directions. When one demon disappeared, another one took its place. The ranks began to thin, but the attacks didn't slow down.

The demon in front of her exploded into nothingness and small blades fell to the ground where he'd stood. She spun around, looking for the next one. There were none. She staggered, and reached out to smear more blood on her wrist.

Gabe grabbed her hand before she could. "Try now."

"What?" She stared at him, trying to figure out what he meant.

He looked towards the graveyard. "I can barely feel the demon in you. Try again now."

Cassidy nodded and struggled to place one foot in front of the other. A shiver went through her and it felt like her skin was attacked by a thousand biting insects, but she was able to enter the graveyard.

Gabe grinned. "I thought so."

Cassidy punched him in the stomach.

Gabe swore, doubling over. "What was that for?"

"He's not my boyfriend."

Gabe burst out laughing, dropping to the ground. Laying back he stared at the stars that were starting to fade in the lightening sky. His laughter faded away and he rubbed his stomach. "Be nice or I won't teach you how to use my blades. If you're lucky I might even show you how to use a few of my other favourites."

Cassidy dropped to the ground beside him, stopping herself from rubbing the burn in her wrist when she saw the blood on her hand. "Which ones."

"Bow, crossbow and shuriken."

"What's the last one?"

"Ninja stars."

Cassidy eyed him. "I didn't hit you that hard." It had been more about making a point, not hurting him. Or at least not hurting him much.

Gabe lifted his shirt. "Is it bruised?" He sat up slightly and checked his stomach. "It feels bruised."

She stared at the expanse of skin above the leather band. She tightened her hand into a fist, keeping it at her side. There were no blades at the front, but she could see a few tucked in the sides of the band.

"You going to kiss it better?" Gabe's lips curved into a smile. "Your… friend can't get me in here."

Cassidy looked away, biting the inside of her lip to hold back her smile. "Grow up."

Gabe rolled to his side, reaching out to wrap his fingers around her arm. When she turned to look at him he appeared serious. "You okay?"

Cassidy nodded.

"Why didn't you call him?" He sat up.

She looked away as he pulled his shirt back into place. "I didn't need him. I had everything under control." Although there had been a few moments where she hadn't been sure about that.

"We had everything under control." Gabe stressed

the first word as he took her left hand and turned so he could see her inner wrist that was smeared with blood. He ran a finger over the wound. "Are you sure you're okay?"

Cassidy nodded, tugging her arm away from him.

"Do you know you're feeding him every time you do that? It'll be making him stronger."

Cassidy shrugged. It didn't make any difference. She couldn't manage without it. She forced her legs to work and rose to her feet. "Ready to go home?"

"Home. Sounds good." He smiled down at her once he was on his feet.

"My home," she corrected before she spun and left the graveyard, relieved to have an end to the sensation of biting insects. Gabe's laughter followed her as she pulled on her helmet and buckled the strap. Then she was forced to wait while he gathered his blades from the ground.

Chapter Fifteen

Cassidy woke starving. She stretched and slowly rose from the bed, yawning as she made her way to the bathroom. Once she was finished in there she considered grabbing a bowl of dry cereal then remembered Gabe's offer to cook. Striding to the spare room, she flung open the door.

He was stretched crossways on the double bed, lying on his back. The sheets were pushed off the end and he wore a pair of black boxer shorts. One arm was above his head, the other flung across the bed.

She stared at him for a few moments, her lips curving into a smile as she thought of what he'd say if he knew she stood there admiring him. He'd never let her forget it. "Gabe." He continued to sleep. She raised her voice. "Gabe." Frowning she came into the room and leaned over him, about to touch him on the shoulder to shake him awake.

He came up off the bed, reaching for a knife on the floor beside him and looming over her. Cassidy felt a rush of energy. She twisted the knife from his hand, throwing him to the side. Rising above him, she held the knife at his throat, sitting astride him as her other hand pressed against his shoulder to pin him to the bed.

Gabe blinked then smiled. "Guess I should have warned you. Think you can move that knife from my throat. I shaved before I went to bed this morning. It was risky enough with a razor and a painted mirror let alone a sharp knife."

Cassidy threw the knife to the floor, but kept him pinned to the bed. "I called you." She refused to acknowledge the mirror comment. It was none of his business why she'd painted them.

"I thought you'd sleep longer. You looked dead on your feet this morning when we got home."

"This is my house, damn it."

"Next time throw something at me."

"A shuriken?"

Gabe laughed and his hands went to her waist. "Maybe I better not teach you how to use any more weapons. I think you're dangerous enough as it is."

Cassidy released him, pulling away from his hands.

"Then you better remember that." She could still feel the warmth of where his hands had been.

Gabe grabbed her wrist before she could move too far away. When she sent a glare his way he spoke. "I'll sleep through anything except something coming into my personal space. My family usually throw a pillow."

Cassidy tugged her arm from his light grip. "I'm not your family."

Gabe sat up and swung his legs over the edge of the bed, his gaze roving over her. "Nope. You certainly aren't." He grinned as he rose to his feet.

Cassidy took a step backwards. "You said you'd cook if you stayed." She looked away when he stretched then rubbed his chest. "You know where the kitchen is." She fled. No, she corrected herself, retreated. She stared at the painted mirror in her bedroom. She ran a fingernail through some of the paint and caught a glimpse of hazel. She blinked. It wasn't time to remove the paint. She turned away from that small glimpse of her eye and leaned back against the mirror. Closing her eyes, she sighed. What the hell was she meant to do? About anything.

"What do you want for breakfast?"

Cassidy opened her eyes to see Gabe standing in the doorway. He was bare-chested, but now wore black jeans. She forced her gaze to move past his chest to meet his green stare. "I don't care. Anything but dry cereal."

"Why dry cereal?"

"Because I always forget to buy milk." Her mum had forgotten to buy milk. It had been the beginning of the end. And then milk just hadn't seemed important to remember.

"We can get some when we go out later."

"No."

"No? You don't want to buy milk?" When she shook her head, he asked, "Then what am I meant to have in my coffee?"

"Buy cream. Or there's ice cream in the freezer. It saves adding sugar." She pushed away from the mirror and strode towards him, stopping when he didn't move.

"So, no milk allowed in the house. You want to tell me why?"

"No. Now get out of my way."

Gabe stared at her a moment longer before he stepped back. "Do you have a spare house key?"

Cassidy had started down the hall. She stopped and turned to face him. "Why?"

"I want to grab my gear from Gran's house."

"You know I never actually said you could stay."

"Of course you did."

"When?"

Gabe grinned at her. "When you didn't slam the door in my face when we came here this morning." He strode towards her. "Breakfast, then I need to get my gear. Think you can drop me over there? I'm sure I can get a lift back. Or should I ring one of my cousins to pick me up?" He draped his arm around her shoulders, taking her to the kitchen with him. "One of my bible bashing cousins. Although they're probably all at church today."

Cassidy rolled her eyes, pulling away from him. "Just what I need around here," she muttered. "Fine. We'll take my car. But you better not have much. It doesn't have a lot of space."

"A couple of duffel bags and a handful of weapons." He pulled a carton of eggs from the fridge. "French toast? With ice cream instead of milk?"

Cassidy stared at the eggs in his hand for a moment before she nodded. "And put a shirt on. If oil from the pan splatters you, it'll burn."

Gabe sent her a knowing look. "Would it make you feel better if I covered up from head to toe? Maybe a full ninja outfit."

"I'm not prancing around the kitchen without a shirt."

Gabe's gaze dropped to her shirt then back to her eyes. His voice lowered. "I dare you."

Cassidy met his gaze, her heart pounding in her ears. She eventually tore her gaze away from his and turned her back on him. "Call me when breakfast is ready." She strode to her bedroom and closed the door. This time she locked it. Leaning against the door, she pressed her hand against her heart, willing it to slow. She should tell him he couldn't stay. There was no way in hell she wanted to risk killing someone else. It might not be by her hands, but she knew what Remedy would do if she gave into a single one of her impulses. She groaned as she slid down the door to sit on the floor. Banging her head against the door once, she closed her eyes as her fingers spun the ring she still wore.

It had better be soon. She didn't know how long before she lost the battle against temptation. Tonight she'd ask Remedy how to track down their enemy. And she needed the words of the ritual. She couldn't help thinking about the pages her father had read from. The ones Remedy had burned until they fell around him in ashes. The binding ritual better be shorter than that one. It had taken him far too long to speak those words. And yet it also hadn't been long enough. Pain arrowed through her as she again heard him begging for help. I'm so sorry. Her eyes remained closed as she waited for Gabe to call her.

Chapter Sixteen

Late that afternoon Cassidy sat in her car at the front of the demon hunters' house. She tapped her fingers on the steering wheel. Why hadn't she told him she'd changed her mind? Talk about crazy. And it wasn't Gabe. She needed to be locked up and the key thrown away. She almost cheered when Gabe stepped outside carrying a duffel bag and a rectangular case that she worried might be too long to fit in her boot. Beside him was Riley carrying another duffel bag and a timber toolbox.

Pulling the lever, Cassidy looked in the other direction. She didn't want to talk to anyone. Especially not someone who might try to talk her out of her plans. When the boot closed again she looked over to see the two hunters clasp left hands against arms so their marks met at the wrist. Riley clapped Gabe on the shoulder and when they broke apart, handed over several gift vouchers to major supermarkets. She couldn't resist smiling at the sound of Gabe's laughter. Riley waved and headed inside.

Gabe dropped onto the front seat after tossing a duffel bag on the back seat and held the gift cards out to her with a grin. "Didn't I tell you they'd give me food, but not money?"

"Are you really sure you want to stay at my place?"

Gabe tossed the cards into her glove box. "Having second thoughts?"

"No."

Gabe stared at her intently. "Really?"

She reluctantly smiled. "I'm way beyond second thoughts."

Gabe grinned. "Good."

"How can having more than second thoughts about something and still doing it be good?"

"Because you didn't jump in blindly. You at least thought about it first." He checked the time on his phone then tucked it away. "Think we can get my gear back to your house before we do any hunting? I'd rather not carry an arsenal around with us all night."

Cassidy started the car. "What do you do if the cops catch you with any of it?" She reversed out onto the street.

"Pray they never do."

She glanced at him. "Seriously?"

"I've got licenses and I'm supposedly in living history groups, but some of this stuff wouldn't pass inspection." He shrugged. "I don't usually cart that stuff with me, but sometimes I risk it."

"And the rest of the hunters?"

Gabe laughed. "Very few of them use weapons that are illegal in Australia. Or were you asking about the overseas ones?"

Cassidy slammed on her brakes having nearly run into the car ahead of her, that had slowed for a red light, during Gabe's comment. "Overseas?"

"You didn't think it was only Australia that had demons, did you?"

She shook her head. "I hadn't really thought." The traffic in front of her started to move again. She swore. "Isn't there anywhere safe?"

"You could become a nun and live your entire life in a convent."

Cassidy sent him a look. "Get real."

"No," Gabe lowered his voice. "You certainly don't belong in a convent."

Cassidy fell silent, thinking it was safer than where the conversation was going. Gabe chuckled, remaining quiet for the rest of the drive. When they reached her home, she parked the car in the garage and left him to bring in his own gear. She retreated to her bedroom and dropped to the carpet to do push ups. Just because she had demon energy to draw on didn't mean she could let herself get out of shape. She needed every advantage possible when fighting demons.

Half an hour later when she was lying on her back staring at the ceiling, sweat soaking her shirt, Gabe knocked on her door. She pushed herself to her feet and unlocked the door, half opening it.

Gabe's gaze travelled over her, pausing at her sweat soaked shirt before he handed her a folded piece of paper. "Learn it." He strode towards the spare room.

Cassidy opened the page and read over some of the words. She stared at them a moment longer before she raced after Gabe. "Is this–" She held the paper up, her question breaking off in mid sentence when she saw the weapons on his bed.

A strung bow lay across the large case, which contained two swords, a dismantled crossbow was on the quilt near two full quivers and sitting on the end of the bed was the open tool chest. Cassidy ran her fingers over the variety of blades in the many open, velvet lined drawers. She didn't know what half of them were called, but she recognised a shuriken.

"You were saying?"

Cassidy raised her head to stare at Gabe. "Do you know how to use all these?" At his nod she dropped her gaze to the weapons again. "Every single one of them?"

"Yeah."

"Why do you need so many? I thought you said you only had a handful of weapons. This is far more than a handful."

"Occasionally I like to get up close and personal." He gestured to the swords. "So I use them. But mostly I like ranged weapons and you can't exactly gather them up during a fight if you run out."

His comment reminded her of the reason she'd run after him. She held out the paper. "Is this the ritual?"

"Yeah."

"Where'd you get it?"

Gabe started tidying his bed. "I wrote it out before I went to sleep, but I wanted to check it was accurate, while I was at Gran's, before I gave it to you."

"How did you check?"

"We've got a lot of books about demons." He unstrung the bow and placed it in the case with the swords before he turned to look at her. "I won't be able to say it for you. You'll have to learn it yourself.

And it's not exactly something you're going to be able to read from a page while you're doing it."

Cassidy stared at the paper in her hand. What the hell was she doing? She was crazy. An image of her father calling Remedy to him came to mind. Crazy must run in her family.

Gabe took a step towards her. "Cass?" When she finally met his gaze, he reached out to her, his fingers brushing across her cheek. "You don't have to bind him. He can't enter your house as long as you keep all the entrances salted. You're safe here."

"Then I've let him make my home a prison. No thanks." She raised her hand that held the paper. "I'm going to learn this off by heart."

"Just don't read it out loud. We were warned against that." Gabe grinned. "I always wondered what it'd do. Not sure I'll ever have the guts to find out though."

"Gabe?"

"Yeah?"

"What happens to sinners when they die according to your family?"

"They go to hell. Which wouldn't be a very good place for a demon hunter to go since that's where they send the demons they banish from earth." He smiled wryly. "Be kind of like throwing a cop in a jail cell with everyone he's caught."

"Are you sure this works?" She shook the paper once. "Absolutely positive?"

"Yeah. It's worked several times before. That's not what you should be worried about. Holding onto the demon until the ritual is finished will be the problem. He's not going to stand there quietly and let you trap him forever."

Cassidy nodded and turned to stare at the doorway, waiting for Remedy who she'd felt enter the house. She tucked the paper into her pocket, not wanting to risk him taking it from her. She stared at him when he stood in the doorway.

"What are you planning?" Remedy's gaze remained on Cassidy.

"I need to know how to find our enemy. As soon as I learn the ritual I'm going to hunt him down and bind him." At least she hoped she could. But even if she failed, it had to be better than sitting around waiting for him to come after her.

"All this so you can kiss a boy," Remedy sneered.

"No, all this so I can be free."

"And what will you do with your freedom?" Remedy asked.

Gabe joined Cassidy, standing beside her. "I have a suggestion."

Cassidy turned towards him. "What?"

"Kiss a boy." Gabe grinned.

"Don't you think of anything else?"

"Sure I do. Like how sharp my blades are and how many arrows I have left and," he glanced towards Remedy. "How many demons I can banish in a day."

"It would take very little to kill you, boy." Remedy moved to stand in front of Gabe. "I could snap your neck in seconds, but the thought of prolonging the agony holds great appeal."

"Enough." Cassidy pulled Gabe back and put her hand up when Remedy would have followed. "How do I track our enemy?"

"I can't help you against him. And if you were to call me to your side when you faced him we would both be lost. You don't understand the power you're going to face. We have roamed the earth for many years. The longer a demon abides here the stronger they grow."

"How long have you both been on Earth?" Gabe asked.

"Since a Roman called us forth to slaughter the family of his enemy," Remedy said.

"Holy hell." Cassidy stared at Remedy, her mind

struggling to grasp how many centuries that would be. "You weren't kidding about forever."

"What's your enemy called?" Gabe asked.

"The name he was summoned to answer, translates to castigate."

"He was a punishment?" When Remedy nodded, Gabe asked, "What did the man do wrong?"

Remedy glanced at Cassidy before his gaze focused on Gabe, his lips twisting into a mirthless smile. "He touched what was not his to touch."

Gabe grinned. "Possession is nine tenths of the law."

"Don't play word games with me, boy."

"Can we get back to my question?" Cassidy interrupted before things could get out of hand again. "How do I track Castigate?"

"Share a hunt with me." Flames leapt high in Remedy's eyes.

"No." Gabe grabbed her shoulder, spinning her to face him. "Don't. He wants to possess you. Take over your body. There's never a guarantee he'll give it back."

Cassidy was torn. "What else can I do?"

"I cannot take you to him. I have already told you this."

Cassidy faced Remedy, Gabe's hand still on her

shoulder. "Don't avoid the question. What other options are there?"

Remedy stared at her before he nodded. "You are learning, Cassidy. A memory. A short meeting of minds so you can learn his signature."

She felt Gabe's fingers tighten on her. There had to be more to this. "Short? Set a period of time." She nearly grinned when she felt Gabe's grip on her relax.

"An hour of your time, no more, maybe less."

Cassidy nodded. "How do we do this?"

"Lie on my bed," Gabe said. "I'll set a timer and if he hasn't let you go, I'm pouring holy water over you." He released her to rummage in his duffel bag, pulling out a water bottle that had the label ripped from it. Someone had drawn a stick figure saint on it with a black marking pen. "This entire bottle." His gaze met Remedy's.

"Noted." Remedy gave a sharp nod before he turned to Cassidy. "Are you satisfied with the terms?"

"You're not to mess with anything else in my head while you're in there. Show me what I need to know to hunt Castigate and then get out of there."

Remedy's lips twisted into a smile. "I wonder if this is what it feels like to be a father. You have learned so much."

Cassidy saw red. Pools of red. And somehow she

had Remedy against a wall, her dagger pressed at his throat, no memory of the action that brought her there. "You're not my father. He's dead." The words were a low growl.

"You should know since it was by your hand."

"You tricked us." She screamed the words.

"I was the one forced to that building. A demon cannot be summoned once he's already on Earth and has completed his task. I was free. Castigate forced that on me by giving your father my name. I had no oaths to fulfil, nothing owed to another. I was free." Flames consumed the black of his eyes.

"Because of you my father's dead." She pressed the blade harder against his throat and felt blood drip along her throat too. Gabe spoke behind her, but none of his words made sense.

"Because your father didn't question the information he was given he's dead. It is always the way. You humans blame us for your own failings."

"You and Castigate are to blame."

"You know nothing. Nothing." Remedy's hand wrapped around her throat. "You want the truth? Would you recognise it or are you too caught up in your own miseries?" He flung her back.

Chapter Seventeen

Cassidy hit the foot of the bed, slumping to the ground. She felt hands on her and brushed them away. Her body ached and she wiped at the blood across her throat. Her gaze stayed on Remedy, blood streaking his throat. "What is the truth?"

"Cass. Cass, please. You're going to get yourself killed." Gabe twisted the dagger from her hand.

She finally turned to him. Pain filled her as she met his gaze. "You know it all. Why aren't you running?"

Gabe wrapped his arms around her, pulling her close. "Because I know nothing. Maybe one day you'll tell me."

Remedy roared behind them, dragging them apart. Energy crackled around him as he pointed a finger at Gabe. "How many times must I warn you?" He stalked forward.

Gabe rose to his feet. "Haven't you ever witnessed

comfort before? Do you think I'd be stupid enough to do more than that while you're watching?"

Cassidy leapt to her feet, throwing herself at Remedy, pounding against his back. "Don't you dare. Leave him be." She was flung to the ground to stare up at Remedy. The world seemed frozen. Silence filled the room. Then a trickle of blood ran down Remedy's throat and Cassidy had the urge to consume it. Revulsion shuddered through her and instead she wiped the blood from her throat across her demon mark. Energy flared. Pain momentarily increased before receding. She rose slowly, her gaze never leaving Remedy's. "Never touch him again. Ib–"

"Do not speak that name to me."

She slowly stalked towards him. "You offered me the truth. Where is it?"

"Cass. No. Not now. Wait till everyone is calm," Gabe protested.

She ignored Gabe, reaching out with her right hand to run a finger across Remedy's throat. He caught her hand, pulling it away. "Well?"

Remedy nodded and released her.

Wondering what Remedy's blood would do, Cassidy ran her bloodstained finger across her demon mark. She tensed at the pain, her lips curving into a smile at the rush of even more energy. It felt like a victory. "Guess that was a little something you weren't going to share."

Remedy shrugged. "It doesn't matter how it enters your body once the bond has been formed. A wound, drinking it." He shrugged again. "It's all the same." He gestured towards the bed. "Are we doing this or are you finding ways to postpone it?"

She walked across the room and lay on the bed beside the weapons that were still on it. She looked up to find Gabe leaning over her, Remedy behind him. "Set your alarm."

"Cass–"

Cassidy interrupted him. "Please, Gabe. Not now."

Gabe stared at her a moment longer before he nodded. He took out his phone and set his alarm before placing it on the bedside table and sitting next to her on the bed. He linked his fingers with hers. "I will watch over you." His gaze went to Remedy. "Now who is wasting time?"

Remedy leaned over Cassidy, his hands reaching out to cup her face, fingertips at her temples. Her gaze was caught by his, red flames overwhelmed by blackness until all was black. Then an image formed.

A woman with long reddish brown hair and dark blue eyes smiled at Remedy. "What would I do without you, Protector? Before my husband summoned you I was afraid to even leave my bed of a morning. How it must bore you to forever trail in my shadow."

"They are the terms I agreed to, Iulia. To protect you and guard you against all men but your husband until the birth of your first child." Remedy returned her smile. It was an easy task and once he had completed it, he would be free to roam the world. Alone. His smile became harder to hold in place.

Iulia's smile faded. "What if I am barren? We have been married two years and still there is no child. I have left offerings to the goddess Diana and she has never answered my pleas."

He wanted to reach out and comfort her. Instead, he remained still. "Then I will guard you till your last days."

Iulia reached out and took his hand. "You always know what to say to cheer me, Protector. I wish I could do the same for you when I see sorrow in your eyes."

"No life is without sorrow." He placed his other hand over hers, cupping it between both of his. "Not yours, not mine." Especially not his.

The scene faded, and reformed.

Iulia was wrapped in Remedy's arms, his lips

pressed against her throat. "My love, please, I would not have you break your terms of service." She tried to pull away from him.

Remedy met her gaze, a smile curving his lips. "This will not break them. I swore to protect you against men. I am a demon." Flames leapt in his eyes at her answering smile.

"The thought of having a child terrifies me, Protector. I would not have you leave me."

"Four years and no child, I think you can stop worrying. But even if you should one day prove fertile I will still remain at your side. No one will take you from me." His arms tightened around her.

"One day time will."

He shook his head. "No. That I will not allow." He smiled. "I will give you my name. With that you will be able to defeat even time itself." His lips met hers.

Again the scene faded to be replaced by another.

Iulia stared up at Remedy with tears in her eyes. "I waited in the hope it wasn't true, but it has been three months now. I am with child, Ibaelcaurzanon."

Remedy pulled her to him, one hand cradling the back of her head. "Why the tears, Iulia?"

"I don't want you to leave me."

Remedy smiled at her, a finger wiping away tears.

"Then stop crying. How many times must I say I will never leave you?"

"But the terms set by my husband are nearly ended. What if you are returned home?"

"It will not happen. Your husband is a fool and didn't say what was to happen to me once the contract was ended. I am free to roam where I please when your child is born. But I have no desire to stray from your side, Iulia. And even if something was to happen to send me home, you have my name and can call me to you."

She wrapped her arms around his neck, her smile radiant as she rose on tiptoes. "I cannot stop thinking that it wasn't until you become my lover that I fell pregnant." She pressed her lips against his, cutting off any words he might have uttered.

His arms tightened around her as he returned her kiss. He'd been thinking the same thing.

When the scene faded and reformed it was Remedy and another man.

"What do you want of me, Castigate?"

"To end the favour I owe you."

"What do you offer?" He wished Castigate would hurry. He had an errand to tend to so he could return to Iulia's side. This close to the birth he'd hated to leave her, but her husband had ordered it and he was bound to follow his orders for a little longer.

"Information about your human lover."

Remedy showed no emotion, but wished he could rip Castigate's tongue from his head for even mentioning Iulia indirectly. Instead he inclined his head. "If it is of sufficient value I will call us even."

"Her husband has found out that you are her lover and plans to have you murdered. She will be put to death once the child is born." Castigate paused. "Providing it looks human the child will be allowed to live."

"When." Remedy had never felt fear before but he had a feeling it was the emotion that now filled him with an almost paralysing power.

"Demons have been called to rend you to pieces. They wait by your lover's bed."

"And where is the human woman?" He couldn't bring himself to speak Iulia's name in Castigate's presence.

Castigate shrugged. "Her husband's soldiers took her away about an hour ago. That's why he sent you on this errand."

Remedy nodded. He had no time to haggle over the worth of information like he should. "Your debt is settled. We are even."

Castigate began to move away when a scream seemed to pierce the air around Remedy. He turned back in time to hear Iulia's voice scream, "Ibaelcaurzanon, run."

Remedy fell to his knees as pain filled him. His hands dug into the dirt, fingers becoming claws as he threw his head back and roared.

Castigate stared down at Remedy. "She is yours? The human? You made her yours? Gave her power over you?"

Remedy rose to his feet, his gaze meeting Castigate's. He spoke no words before he pictured Iulia in his mind and transported himself as close as he could. It wasn't close enough. Her and her husband were in the middle of a salt circle. Two guards with them, holding Iulia up between them. Remedy roared when he saw the sword driven through her stomach, the child dead at her feet, furled wings at its back.

"Do what you must, my love." Her voice faded as she slumped, only held from the ground by the guards.

He knew she meant run and survive, but more than that, he needed to avenge her. And needed to hold her in his arms. Remedy's gaze sought out the man who'd called him to this world. He was no longer his master. The child had been born. "You will die. Slowly. Painfully."

"You broke the contract," the man screamed at him.

Remedy shook his head. "No man but you touched her in all the years I protected her. And if it wasn't for the contract I would have cut your hands from your body the first time you did."

"I have called demons to deal with you. They will tear you into shreds and scatter you from one end of Rome to the other. I will feed parts of you to my dogs for daring to ever touch my wife. For forcing her to bear your unnatural progeny."

Remedy felt the demons the moment they entered the room and turned to face them, pain and anger filling him with their power. "I give you fair warning, brothers. What has been asked of you I shall do instead. If you left an escape in your contracts use it now."

Chapter Eighteen

The demons launched themselves at Remedy, laughing at his words. Remedy relished their choice. He wanted to tear the room apart. He made do with tearing into the demons instead. When he finally turned back to the circle of salt he was covered in demon blood. His anger and pain were not diminished in the slightest.

His gaze was drawn to Iulia who now lay on the floor with their child. He strode to the edge of the circle of protection. He yearned to cross it and take her in his arms. She still lived, barely. He turned his attention to the two guards who stared at him, wide eyed with fear. He pointed at each of them.

"I have marked you for death. There is only one means to escape my punishment." His gaze fell to the salt before returning to the guards. "Break the circle."

The two fought to be the first to comply, dusting

away at the precious commodity with trembling hands. Behind them Iulia's husband screamed abuse at them, trying to pull them away from their task. Remedy watched as they ran from the room, leaving a path to Iulia.

He knelt at her side, gently pulling her into his arms. "Iulia."

She looked up at him, reaching out with a blood stained hand to touch his face. "I love you, my protector."

"I failed you."

"No. We were betrayed." Her eyes closed as her hand fell to her side.

Remedy roared as he felt her life slip away. He pulled her tight against him, pressing his lips to hers before he laid her gently on the ground, drawing the sword from her body. He turned to face the man who cowered in the corner of the room. Remedy strode towards him, the sword dripping blood onto the floor. Losing control of his human shape, his wings snapped out around him.

"Please. It wasn't my plan. Castigate came to me. He offered me the information only if I promised to do something with it."

"Castigate." Remedy shook his head. "No."

"It was your own fault, brother."

Remedy turned to face Castigate who had entered the room at the sound of his name. "Why?"

"How many times did I try and offer you something to make things even between us? None of it was good enough. You would have kept me in your shadow for a millennium. Now though," his lips twisted into a smile. "I can keep you in my shadow, Ibaelcaurzanon."

Self preservation warred with revenge. "This is not over." Remedy spun, dropped the sword and lifted Iulia's husband, snapping his neck. He raced into the night, wishing he could have taken Iulia and the child with him. But he didn't have time, not if he wanted to live. He held the signature of Castigate in his mind. He'd be able to find him anywhere. If he could overcome the problem of a true name in the wrong hands. Somehow he would avenge Iulia and their child. Hate burned in him as he continued to flee, putting as much space as possible between him and Castigate.

Cassidy came back to herself, with tears and Remedy's hands still on her face. She met his gaze, the pain still filling his eyes. She placed her hands over his. "I'm sorry. I'm so sorry." It was a relief to finally be able to speak the words. Even if they were spoken to the wrong person.

Remedy pulled away from her like he'd been struck, then Gabe was there, wrapping his arms around her. "Are you okay? Cass? What happened?" He brushed at her tears with his palm. "Cass?" His green eyes stared at her intently.

She blinked, unable to speak. Instead she slid her arms around him and pressed her head to his chest. Remedy watched her from where he stood beside the bed. Flames flickered in his eyes and energy crackled in the air. I'm sorry. The words echoed over and over again in her head, the taste of Remedy's truths on her lips. She squeezed her eyes shut and bit back a sob as she felt both her loss and his. Iulia! Dad! She wanted to scream for both of them.

"Cass."

The concern in Gabe's voice pulled her away from the overwhelming grief as she struggled to gain control. "I'm okay. I'm okay." She shuddered as she tried to convince herself. Her eyes opened and she looked up at him, pulling away slightly. "I'm okay." She drew away from him, still sitting on the bed. She could feel Remedy behind her, his gaze still on her. She had no words for Gabe, but she did need to speak to Remedy. Sliding off the bed, she held a hand out to him.

Remedy stared at her hand for a moment before he

took it and tugged her forward. He remained silent, staring intently at her.

"I can't forgive what you did. But I hate him too. For both of us."

Remedy's fingers tightened on hers before he nodded.

"But don't expect me to like you. If I ever liked you I'd have to hate myself."

"Sometimes the one you blame isn't the one who deserves it."

"You were still partly responsible."

"So were you." He released her hand and walked away.

Cassidy watched him go, her feelings for him a confusing mess. As she felt him leave the house she became aware of another sense. Castigate's signature burned within her. She could tell exactly where he was. The direction. The distance. Anger rushed through her, demon energy on its heels. She turned to face Gabe. "I can find him."

Gabe swore, crossing the room in seconds. "Don't lose yourself, Cass. You have demon eyes."

She pulled away from him, turning to the mirror that was painted over, refusing to believe his words. She ran fingernails over the paint but it didn't help enough.

"Here." Gabe handed her a shaving mirror, a toiletry bag and contents now scattered on the bed. He pushed it towards her. "Take it."

Cassidy's fingers hesitantly touched the mirror. It had been so long since she'd wanted to look in one. And she'd only used a mirror once since painting over them the first week after… her world had changed. She slowly raised it, noticing her jagged reddish brown hair, pale tear-streaked face and the blood at her throat. She took a deep breath and forced herself to meet her own gaze. In the hazel depths of her eyes was a flicker of flame. She jumped back, dropping the mirror as if it had burned her.

Gabe leapt forward and snatched the mirror from the air before it hit the ground. He tossed it onto the bed before he pulled her towards him, wrapping his arms tight around her. "Shh. It's okay."

It was then she realised she was crying. "No. It's not. It'll never be okay." Her voice broke on a sob. "I killed him. I killed my own father." And then she told him everything, through sobs and tears and gasps of pain.

He drew her back to the bed, his arms still tight around her, and told her over and over again that everything would be okay. But she didn't believe him. How could anything ever be okay again? She fell asleep in his arms, exhausted.

Chapter Nineteen

Cassidy slowly woke, pressed against a warm body, an arm flung over her. She stilled as she realised she was beside Gabe who was dressed only in boxers. Moving her head, she found the bed was empty of everything but them. Even the bedding was missing, except for the fitted sheet beneath them. Recalling last time she'd tried to wake Gabe, Cassidy wondered if it was safe to move. She tried to inch away from him and his arm tightened on her. She froze.

Gabe's head lifted and he stared blearily at her. "What's wrong?"

"No daggers this morning?"

"No." He frowned. "You were worried about that?"

"You have to admit that last time I woke you wasn't exactly a typical event."

"Sorry. It's different if I'm expecting someone in my personal space."

"How do you know that?"

Gabe laughed. "How do you think I know?" He grinned. "Remember, I've never aspired for sainthood."

"You could have told me instead of leaving me to worry you'd murder me before I could get out of bed."

"Do you think I can claim a kiss under the heading of comforting and not die a horrible death?"

"You still want to kiss me?"

"Why wouldn't I?" Gabe leaned over her. "Well?"

"I'm a murderer."

"I nearly killed my sister when I was ten-years-old."

"It's not the same." She paused, then asked, "You have a sister?"

Gabe nodded. "Two of them. And it is the same. I wanted to go on a school camp."

"You tried to kill her on a school camp? Around other people?"

"Will you shut up and let me tell the story?"

"Fine," Cassidy muttered.

"She wasn't on the school camp with me. But there was a demon in the area who thought it'd be entertaining to play with a demon hunter's child. Luckily my mum had sent someone to keep an eye on me. I would have protested if I'd known because at ten-years-old I knew I could look after myself. Afterwards," he fell silent for a bit. "Afterwards I had nightmares for years."

"What has that got to do with your sister? She wasn't even in the story."

"Not very patient are you? I can relate to that sometimes." Gabe grinned at her. "Like when someone makes me wait days for the kiss they're going to give me."

Cassidy's heart leapt and she wanted to tell him to stop talking and just do.

"Whoa, demon girl. You're eyes are doing that flame trick again."

Cassidy closed her eyes. "Get on with the story then."

"You're the one who interrupted." He ran his finger along her nose, over the tip and stopped when he reached her lips.

"Gabe." Her voice was a whisper as she opened her eyes to look up at him.

The intensity of his gaze increased before he moved away, lying on his back beside her. "You're right."

Cassidy sat up so she could see his expression. "About what?"

Gabe shook his head. "I was telling you a story. About my sister."

"Who isn't in the story," Cassidy pointed out.

"You know how I attacked you when you woke me?" Gabe waited for her to nod before he continued. "Joanna is a year younger than me and a couple of months after the school camp she came running into my room to wake me. I'd taken to sleeping with a knife under my pillow and when she jumped on my bed I attacked her."

Cassidy waited for him to continue. He didn't. "What happened?"

"There was blood everywhere. And she screamed so loud the neighbours probably heard her. They lost her on the operating table. Twice. And she was in hospital for months." His lips slowly smiled. "And she made me her slave for years. Every time I wouldn't do what she wanted she'd say it was only fair since I'd nearly killed her." He chuckled softly. "She pulled that trick on me when I didn't want to go to Charlotte's wedding. So in a way it's her fault I'm stuck in Brisbane." He reached up to run a finger down the middle of her lips to stop on her chin. "I'll have to thank her for that."

"This happened eleven years ago."

Gabe nodded. "Yeah."

"And you're still expecting to be attacked in your sleep. What did the demon do?" Cassidy squealed when Gabe rolled, pushing her back so she was again below him.

The silence stretched out. "I was the only person who walked away from that camp alive."

"Gabe–" her voice broke as she imagined what that must have been like.

"Shh. It's in the past." His lips brushed across hers and he pulled back with a smile. "Maybe those demon eyes aren't so bad after all. I think I'm starting to learn how to read them."

"Stop staring at me." She closed her eyes.

Gabe's lips brushed her cheek, stopping near her ear. "Why? At least your eyes aren't afraid to tell me what you want."

Cassidy pushed him away and he let her. She sat up, glaring down at him. "You must be crazy. This," she pointed to him then her then him again. "Isn't going to happen. Not when Remedy could psych out and kill you. And regardless of what you think my eyes are telling you I'm not about to put your life in danger for a stupid bloody kiss."

Gabe grinned. "I guess that means sex is out of the question then."

Cassidy growled in frustration and looked around for something to throw at him. Instead she noticed the time and yelped, leaping from the bed. "It's almost dark." She backed away from Gabe, an accusing finger pointed at him. "Don't you dare get yourself killed in front of me. I've seen more than enough death."

Gabe rose from the bed, stepping forward each time she stepped away. "I know what time it is. I don't need a clock to tell me. And you shouldn't either." He pointed to her wrist. "That should be telling you that you've got about an hour left till sunset."

Cassidy frowned as she stared at her wrist. "How?"

"You need to be more aware of what's happening. Not just around you, but in you. A hunter only survives by developing all their abilities, including instinct." He took one last step and reached out to put a hand on her back, tugging her forward. He smiled. "I won't tell if you don't." His lips met hers and time slowed to a crawl.

When Gabe pulled away, Cassidy stared up at him. "Crazy," she whispered, but her lips curved into a smile.

Gabe matched her smile. "Your eyes are nearly all fire. How about we skip clubbing once we bind Castigate and spend the night at home?"

Cassidy laughed as she pushed him away from her. "Nice try." She spun away, heading for the bathroom. When she closed the door behind her, she was surprised to find she was still smiling. Thoughts of her father crept in and stole the smile, but it slowly returned as an image of her father swinging her mum around the lounge room came to mind. Her father elated he'd got a promotion. Her mum wanting to go out to celebrate. He'd suggested staying in. Years later she couldn't remember who'd won.

She stepped forward to the sink, gazing at the painted mirror. She scratched away some of the paint, glimpsing a flicker of flame. A little more scratching revealed hazel to go with it. Her father's eyes. Her eyes. No accusation. Just eyes. She stared a moment longer before she turned on the tap and leaned forward to splash water over her face. After she'd dried her face, she checked which direction Castigate was in. She wanted to see if she could track him. Obviously she wasn't ready to take him on, but she needed to know if she had the skill to find him.

Leaving the bathroom, she headed for the kitchen

where she could hear Gabe preparing food. If he didn't want to go with her, she'd go on her own.

Chapter Twenty

Cassidy pulled over to the side of the road to focus on checking the direction again. He'd moved east this time. Didn't Castigate ever stay still?

"Let me ride. We'll never catch him if you've got to keep stopping to find him," Gabe said.

"We're not trying to catch him tonight. How many times have I got to tell you that? I still haven't learned the ritual. I just need to figure out this tracking thing. And stop asking to ride my bike. You don't have a license."

"So? Neither do you."

"Fine. Get off and let me swap places with you," Cassidy snapped. "And if you get caught don't go whining to me."

Gabe chuckled as he hopped off the bike, quickly swapping places with her. He looked over his shoulder at her. "I bet you could Remedy the problem."

"You're not amusing you know." She placed her hands on his hips. "Now move it. He's headed east."

They fell into a pattern, Cassidy's hand tightening on his hip when she wanted him to turn that way. Both hands finally tightening as she yelled, "Stop."

"What's wrong?"

"He's changed direction and headed this way. Move. Now."

Gabe turned the motorbike and gunned the engine, leaning forward.

"Faster." Cassidy's arms encircled his waist as she plastered her body against his. "He's moving quicker than us." She felt the motorbike speed up and closed her eyes. She didn't know what would be worse. Coming off a motorbike at high speed or the demon catching them. Dark energy tracked her and she figured out that coming off the motorbike would be preferable. The demon following them was after her, hunting her in the same way she'd hunted him. She swore. Why hadn't Remedy told her Castigate would feel her hunting him? She felt the motorbike slowing and opened her eyes, about to demand what he was doing. The graveyard was ahead.

Gabe stopped just before the entrance. "Hurry up.

Try. Your demon energy isn't that strong right now." He tugged her towards the graveyard the moment they were off the motorbike, one hand pulling his helmet off.

"I can't." Pain shot through her when she reached the edge and she recoiled from it. "Damn it." She pulled away from him, yanking her helmet from her head to drop it on the ground. Then Castigate was behind her and she spun to face him, pulling out her daggers.

Castigate laughed, the sound echoing through the night. "You think you can face me with those bits of metal?"

Cassidy tended to agree with him, but she wasn't about to tell him that. She tilted her chin and smiled. "I wouldn't have pulled them out if I didn't think so."

Castigate launched himself at her and at the same moment Gabe wrapped his arms around her waist and dragged her into the graveyard. Castigate's howl echoed her scream of pain. She fought Gabe, struggling to leave the graveyard and the pain it caused.

Gabe swore, twisting one of her blades from her hand. "Cass. Enough. You're safe."

She smelt blood, then saw it, a thin line on Gabe's arm from one of her daggers. Reaching out, she instinctively pressed her demon mark against his blood. Pain exploded through her and she was able to pull away from Gabe who echoed her earlier scream, rubbing the rest of the blood from his arm with the edge of his shirt.

Cassidy stared at him on the ground, pain radiating from him. Her own pain causing her to sway on her feet. She wanted to run. To stay. She was torn between escaping the pain and helping Gabe. Under her skin she felt her demon mark twist and writhe, sharp blades of pain striking her with every movement.

Gabe staggered to his feet. "Cass. Please." He reached out his hand. "Drop your dagger."

She looked down at the blade, blood staining its surface. Gabe moved and her gaze returned to him. Behind her she could hear Castigate demanding she face him. Gabe's hand touched her and she let the dagger fall to the ground with a dull thud. Then his arms were around her.

"Let go, Cass. The energy. The blood. Let it go. You're safe here." His hand rubbed her back, the other pressed her head against his shoulder. "You're safe. I've got you."

Cassidy shuddered, pain slowly ebbing until it was only a million little stings against her skin. Her arms came up to hold him closer against herself. "Your blood. I didn't m-"

"Shh. Don't worry about it." His hand continued to stroke her back. "It's over now."

Cassidy pulled away from him. "No, it's not." She turned in his embrace to see Castigate waiting for her.

"What does he want?" Castigate demanded the moment Cassidy's attention was on him.

"Who?"

"Your master."

Cassidy didn't bother correcting him. It wasn't any of his business. "Nothing. I was curious when I saw his memories."

Castigate grinned. "He was always a fool. Are you his new love to replace the last one I took from him? Tell him your days are numbered too. This time it will be by my hand, not a human's."

"Why? What did he ever do to you?"

"He tried to keep me from my full power. No demon can fully grow in power when they have obligations to others. He stole power that should have been mine by not releasing that hold over me. Now I will steal his when I tear him apart. But you," he pointed at her. "Will be first. I will leave you to slowly die in a pool of your own blood. Bit by bit as I take your blood and power for my own. He weakens himself sharing some of his power with you. But it won't help. You'll still die like the last one." Castigate laughed. "You will all die." He spun away, leathery wings stretching as he took to the air.

Cassidy pulled away from Gabe and staggered to the edge of the graveyard. She dropped to the ground just outside the sanctuary. Gabe joined her, his hand reaching for hers. They remained silent, staring at each other. Cassidy started to tremble.

She swore, wiping a hand across her face. "What have I done? I am so dead."

Gabe's fingers tightened on hers. "We'll figure something out."

There was another rush of air above them and Remedy landed on the ground near Cassidy. "What were you thinking?"

"I haven't got a clue." Cassidy tilted her head back to look at him.

Remedy reached out to drag her to her feet, a hand around her arm. He put his face close to hers. "Then how do you think you're going to win against him if you don't think? Are you trying to get us killed?"

Cassidy shook her head. "I didn't know he'd be so powerful. You said he was like you."

"He is like me. Can't you see?"

Cassidy gasped as power blazed forth from

Remedy. More power than she'd ever seen him display. "I didn't know."

Remedy's head came up as his power dropped to a hum. "I hope you liked that little display because every demon within the city is now headed this way. Hold on you fool." His wings snapped out and he sent a look to Gabe. "You're on your own, boy. You're nothing to me." He launched himself into the air, Cassidy held tight in his grasp.

With a squeal, she wrapped her arms around him at they streaked through the night. It seemed only minutes before Remedy landed outside her window and let her go.

He gestured to the house. "Get inside before they track you down. I should have known you'd be trouble." His hands reached out and tugged on a strand of her hair. "What could I expect with colour like that?" He took to the air again, leaving Cassidy staring up at him.

She felt the energy in the night. Demons seeking the power that had flared out over the city. Sliding open her window, she climbed in, dropping to a heap on the floor. Her arms wrapped around herself and she nearly screamed when the house phone rang.

Staggering to her feet, she checked the time on her bedside clock. Who'd be ringing at two in the morning? Making her way unsteadily to the lounge room she picked up the phone. "Yeah?"

"Thank God you're safe."

"Gabe?"

"Who else rings you at this time of the morning?"

"Oh, Gabe." Her legs gave out and she dropped into the closest armchair. "I'll drive over–"

"Don't be an idiot. You're safe. Stay there."

"What about you?"

"I'll be right if I don't die of boredom. Now if these demons would come a little closer I could use a few more of them for target practice. A pity I don't have my crossbow with me. That'd get the ones hanging back."

"I didn't want to leave you. I didn't have a choice."

"I know. But it's better he took you home. Although I can tell you those first two times I rang and no one answered were the longest minutes of my life."

Cassidy had no clue what to say. Apologise again? Yell at him for being stupid enough to want to go hunting with her?

"You still there, Cass?"

"Yeah."

"I'll be home after dawn." He paused a moment. "It's probably time I got my own motorbike license."

"And your own motorbike?"

"Why would I want that? Riding together is about the only time Remedy lets me have my hands on you. Stay home, Cass. I'll be there soon." He disconnected.

Cassidy dropped the phone on the floor, a smile lingering on her face. She shook her head as she rose to her feet, unsteady legs barely holding her up. "I swear he's got a one track mind," she muttered, heading for the bathroom. Maybe a shower would make her feel better.

It did, but not by much. Dressed in a pair of soft shorts and a singlet, both black, she wandered to Gabe's room with the ritual clutched in her hand. She read it over and over again, drifting off to sleep some time before Gabe arrived home.

She woke to find him kneeling beside the bed, staring at her. His skin was still a little damp from a shower and his chest bare. "Gabe?" The expression on his face scared her. He looked haunted.

He reached out and gently touched her face, running his hands along her neck, shoulders and arms. He ran them back up again, cupping her face. "You're safe." He dragged her against his chest.

Cassidy felt the pound of his heart against her and slid her arms around him. "Yeah. I'm safe." She felt his arms tighten on her and she pulled him towards her. "Sleep. We'll worry about it all in the morning."

Gabe lay down beside her, still holding her tight against him. "I didn't know if he was trying to save you or had finally lost control and was going to kill you."

"Shh. He's not suicidal. Yet. Go to sleep. You look like crap." She heard the rumble of his laughter through his chest.

"Thanks. I appreciate the compliment."

"I think your ego is big enough without me feeding it."

"How about tomorrow night we stay home and I teach you how to use some of the toys in my toolbox?"

"Hiding?"

"No. Come on, Cass. One night. It's not hiding. Learning is just as important as going out there and letting them all think you're fearless."

"You'll teach me how to throw your shuriken?"

"Yeah. If you want."

"I should practice the ritual." She suddenly realised she'd fallen asleep reading it. She tried to pull away from him. "My ri-"

"I put it on the bedside table."

She relaxed against him. "Thanks." He didn't

answer. The only sound she heard from him was the beating of his heart against her ear. She fell asleep to that sound.

Chapter Twenty-One

Gabe dropped a scoop of ice cream into his coffee cup before he turned to Cassidy. "So where can we train? Before you make a decision let me point out the walls will probably need repairing and repainting before you've learned how to use all my weapons." He stirred the ice cream into his coffee, his gaze still on Cassidy who was at the kitchen table with a plate of eggs, fried tomatoes and toast.

"I don't know."

He took a sip of his coffee and placed his cup on the kitchen counter he leaned against. "What about the other bedroom."

"No." She drew in a shaky breath, trying to calm herself after shouting the word at him.

"Whoa." He held up a hand. "Give me a chance to remove the dagger from my side."

"Shut up," she muttered.

"What's in there?"

Cassidy ignored him as she ate the rest of her breakfast. Once she was finished, she looked up to see he still watched her, sipping his coffee. She shook her head. "No." This time she managed to say the word calmly.

"I didn't say anything."

She pushed away from the table. "Yeah, but I know you now. You just go ahead and do what you want anyway. Or keep at someone until they give in. Like water on a stone."

"Self-defence against your stubbornness."

Cassidy spun away without replying. She stalked towards her bedroom, stopping when she reached the room in question. She placed her hand on the timber door, looking at the large nails she'd hammered through the door and into the frame at an angle. She felt Gabe come to a stop behind her, but let the silence stretch out. She finally turned to meet his gaze.

"They're not coming back."

"I know." Her words were as quiet as his.

"We could empty out the garage," he offered.

She shook her head, leaning against the door. "There's a hammer in the bottom kitchen drawer."

"Well of course, everyone knows that's where you keep them."

She smiled slightly. "I needed to break some ice."

He grinned. "Perfectly logical." He held out his hand. "Let's go and get it then."

She stared at his hand. A mixture of smooth skin, calluses and faint scars. She rubbed her thumb across her own fingers and the top of her palm. Already she had calluses. Reaching out her hand she took his. "Okay." She liked how he didn't automatically want to take over, even with his pushiness. Liked that he believed she was as capable as him at doing things.

"Although if those nails are as long as they look you're on your own with your demon strength. A mere mortal can't be expected to remove a nail as long as the Great Wall."

Cassidy laughed. "Wuss." They reached the kitchen and she let go of his hand to retrieve the hammer. Her laughter faded when she was again facing the bedroom door. She took a deep, unsteady breath, her fingers tightening around the handle of the hammer. When Gabe's hand rested on her shoulder, she turned to look at him.

He met her gaze for several seconds before he smiled. "How about I do the top ones and you do the ones at the bottom since you're shorter than me."

"I'm not that much shorter." She shrugged off his hand and put the claw of the hammer around a nail and levered it out. The nail dropped to the ground and she started on the next one. Her vision blurred as she removed it.

Gabe reached past her and took the hammer. "I thought we were sharing the job. Must be my turn." He guided her out of the way, a hand on her waist. "Typical," he muttered. "You had to let me be the one kneeling on the ground, didn't you?" He knelt in front of the door. "You're probably going to expect me to kiss your feet too while I'm down here." He levered a nail from the door.

Cassidy wiped the back of her hand across her eyes and joined him on the floor. When he turned to look at her, she reached for the hammer. He hesitated then with a nod of his head handed it over. "Thank you." She continued to meet his gaze.

"Isn't that my line since I'm getting out of the chore?"

"Move over." She quickly finished pulling out the last few nails once he moved then stared at the door, wondering if she had the strength to open it.

Gabe's hands rested on her shoulders. "How about we go clean out the garage?"

She shook her head. "It's just a room."

He helped her to her feet. "Don't give me that crap.

Do you know how long it was before I could sleep in my bedroom after I nearly killed my sister?"

"How long?"

"I'll let you know when I finally do."

She opened her mouth then closed it, shaking her head in disbelief. "Now who's speaking crap?"

Gabe grinned. "I'm serious. I moved into the lounge room, refused to go back in that room and my mum just closed the door and told me to let her know when I wanted it back again. When I was at uni I moved in with some mates." He shrugged, "It was like the room didn't exist anymore. None of us even thought about it after a while. Like there was nothing beyond the door but a black hole."

Her look of disbelief increased. "You went to uni?"

Gabe threw back his head and laughed. The sound filled the hallway and he pulled her to him, wrapping his arms around her. "Out of all I've said you find that the hardest to believe?"

"Then why are you stuck here if you don't even live with your family normally? What about work?"

"I work for my family, hunting demons. And Mum took all my ID home with her. She only left me with my phone. I'm working on getting stuff sent to me. It isn't easy to prove who you are without references.

And it's not the kind of thing I'd tell my mates. I'd never hear the end of it."

"What is going on here?"

Cassidy tried to pull away from Gabe at the sound of Remedy behind her. All she was able to do was turn in his arms to face the demon. She sighed. "Is that all you can ever say?"

"When all he ever does is place his hands on you then that is all I can say." His gaze went over her head to Gabe. "Now get your hands off her. You are trying my patience, human."

Gabe's arms dropped away from Cassidy. "Do you have to interrupt every quiet moment? Where were you when we were facing down demons?"

"It is the quiet moments that are the most worrying. When she's fighting demons I can feel her life flowing through her."

Cassidy winced. "I think I've had enough of this conversation." She turned and flung the bedroom door open. Anything was better than listening to unnerving comments from Remedy. She took a single step into the room. A rush of memories hit her. Running in to wake her parents on Christmas morning and bouncing on their bed. Playing with her mum's jewellery, which she kept in the crystal containers on her duchess, when she was almost a teenager. Wobbling around in her mum's high heels when she was in preschool.

Gabe rested a hand on her shoulder. "Do you want everything moved out or set to one side?"

The warmth of his hand and the tone of his voice dragged her back to the present. "One side. I guess. Maybe at the window."

"What are you planning?" Remedy demanded.

She was tempted to leave Remedy wondering, but Gabe had already annoyed him enough. "A practice room. Gabe is going to show me how to use his weapons."

"You will need something for a target." Remedy gestured towards the mattress. "You could use that."

Cassidy stared at it for a moment before she nodded sharply and strode forward to strip dusty linen from the bed. Along with the duchess, bedside drawers and wardrobe, the linen was moved to the wall with the window. Once the mattress stood against the wall, ready to be used as a target, the bed base joined the rest of the items. Cassidy stared at the mattress before she strode from the room to her own bedroom. Rummaging in a drawer she pulled out a permanent marker and turned to find Gabe watching her from the doorway. She held up the marker.

Gabe's smile contained relief. "You draw a bullseye while I grab some weapons."

Cassidy nodded. She reached the doorway but he still stood there so she couldn't pass. "What's wrong?"

"Are you okay?"

Cassidy thought for a moment then nodded. "I think so." She hesitated. "But if I'm not, I will be."

Gabe grinned. "Good." He stepped out of the way. "Give me a minute and I'll show you a whole new definition of fun." He stepped close. "And once we get rid of Castigate I'll show you yet another one."

Cassidy couldn't help laughing as she pushed him away. "Let's start with the weapons and I'll see what I think about your first definition of fun before I even consider thinking about the second definition." She strode down the hallway, feeling his gaze on her. She glanced his way as she turned and entered her parents' room. No, the training room. It was much easier to think of it that way.

Chapter Twenty-Two

By the time Cassidy had finished drawing a bullseye on the mattress, Gabe was back with his toolbox. He set it on the floor against the wall opposite the mattress and opened it. He looked up at her. "What do you want to start with first?"

Cassidy shrugged. "I don't know. The ones you seem to use the most. The little ones."

Gabe rose to his feet with a handful of blades. He stood near her, opposite the mattress, and gave her a quick lecture then a demonstration. His blade hit the centre of the bullseye and he handed a blade to her. She looked down at it and mentally shrugged as she threw it. She came nowhere near her target. She frowned. It wasn't as easy as it looked. Taking the next blade Gabe handed her, she took careful aim. She nearly growled in frustration. Remedy did. She glanced at him where he stood in the doorway, arms crossed. After a glare, she took another blade from Gabe. This time she didn't bother aiming. It hadn't helped last time. She might as well close her eyes for all the difference it made.

"I can't watch this," Remedy muttered.

"Then go away." She took another blade and threw it at the mattress again, wincing when she was still nowhere near the target. "They just don't feel right."

Remedy strode towards her. "Of course they feel right. You are the problem." He reached out to cup her face, his fingers at her temple.

"What are you doing?" Cassidy tried to pull away.

"Putting me out of my misery. Now shut up." Remedy's fingers tightened on her.

"She didn't agree to this," Gabe argued.

Cassidy opened her mouth to agree with Gabe, but she was swallowed up in the blackness of Remedy's eyes. Then image after image bombarded her like physical blows. Sensation, weight, feel, action. Weapon after weapon in her hands, used correctly. Daggers thrown fluidly from her fingers, arrows let loose to hit targets, swords swung at opponents, numerous guns fired and staves wielded expertly. She stumbled backwards, running into the wall of her parents' room, gasping for breath as her ears seemed to ring with sound.

Hands reached for her, supporting her when her legs would have given out. Then the sounds became intelligible and she heard Gabe calling her name.

"I'm okay." She tried to straighten and the room spun around her. "I think."

"Do you want to sit down?" Gabe peered at her intently.

Cassidy shook her head. Then winced when the room spun again. "Give me a minute."

"Here." Remedy shoved a glass of liquid at her.

Cassidy peered into it, sniffing the contents.

Remedy growled. "It is water from your own fridge. Do you think I would kill you off after all that effort?"

Cassidy sipped and felt more centred. Her body began to feel more her own and not like something that was too small for her frame. She pulled away from Gabe and turned her attention to Remedy. "What effort?"

Remedy took the glass from her and handed over one of Gabe's small blades. "Centre yourself. Feel the blade. Use the memory. Then throw."

"Okay." She drew the word out as she turned away from Remedy, wondering if demons could become mentally unstable or if that was a normal state for them. She took a deep breath and felt the blade in her hand. A sense of familiarity rushed through her. She knew how to throw this, had thrown ones just like it a million times before. No, not her. Her mouth dropped open as she turned stunned eyes to Remedy.

He reached out and tapped under her chin to make her mouth close. "Now throw it properly. Not like you've closed your eyes and crossed your fingers."

Cassidy grinned at the fairly accurate description of her earlier attempts. With a nod she faced the mattress and the blade flew true. A buzz of excitement raced through her when she hit the bullseye. "Yes!" She punched the air and grabbed a shuriken. Again familiarity filled her and she threw, barely needing to aim. Her grin widened as she turned to Remedy. "Thank you."

Remedy nodded. "Now try and not get yourself killed."

Her grin faded. "Thank you."

"What for this time?" Remedy asked.

"Reminding me that I'm supposed to hate you." She glared at him. "You stabbed my father."

Remedy sneered. "But you were the one who killed him."

"Whoa." Gabe grabbed her around the waist when she would have attacked Remedy. "Calm down.

Everything's okay. Well, as much as it can be when you're buddying up with a demon."

"Like I had much of a choice," Cassidy snarled.

"There is always choice," Remedy said.

"Dying is not a choice." She stopped trying to break free of Gabe's grip.

"It is always a choice. It doesn't have to be one you like, but it is still a choice," Remedy said.

She sagged in Gabe's arms. "Go away, Remedy. I can't deal with you tonight."

"You are staying in?"

Cassidy answered Remedy's question with a nod. He stared at her a moment longer before he turned and left. Cassidy pressed a hand to her mouth when she wanted to call out after him.

"This is too confusing." She faced Gabe. "How can he want to kill me one day and the next help me?"

"Demons aren't like humans. They think on a whole other level. It doesn't matter what is done between them as long as things are kept equal. Once payback is made, as long as all is even between them, then it is left at that. But if one of them thinks things aren't still equal then it will continue. And a demon can hold a grudge for a very long time." He ran his forefinger down her lips to stop on her chin. "Want to take a break?"

She shook her head, dislodging his finger. "No. I want to try every weapon then I'm going to read the ritual until it's time for bed." She reached for another blade.

"Which bed?"

Cassidy sent him a sidelong glance. He grinned at her. She shook her head and threw the blade at the target. Satisfaction bloomed at her accuracy. She wondered what else Remedy could teach her. She pushed that thought aside. When she figured out how to deal with Remedy then she might ask him. For now it was all too confusing.

"Are you even thinking about answering my question?" Gabe handed her another blade.

"Nope."

"It might be the safest place to be. At least you don't have to worry about how dangerous it is to wake me."

"But what about the danger to you? Remedy was very specific in his instructions."

"He's never about during the day and what he doesn't know won't hurt him."

Cassidy took another blade from him, staring at him for a moment. "Don't you ever worry about dying?"

"No more than most people."

"Why not? I mean, you hunt demons for crying out loud. Aren't you terrified each time will be your last?"

He shook his head. "Not terrified. But yeah, I do wonder. But then anything could happen. At least with hunting demons I've got the skills to stand a chance against them." He nodded towards the blade still in her hand. "You going to throw that or would you rather try a bow now?"

Cassidy barely glanced at the target before she threw the blade, turning back to Gabe once it struck dead centre. "I want to try a bow next. And then how about those swords of yours?"

Gabe laughed. "If anyone ever shows you where to buy all this gear I'm going to hide all your bank cards from you. They wouldn't have any stock left once you'd finished."

"I don't need to know where to buy this stuff from. I just tell Remedy what weapons I need and he leaves them on the kitchen table for me." She took the bow and arrow, the familiarity of it settling into her body. Maybe she had a chance against Castigate after all. Letting the arrow fly towards the target she grinned as it hit dead centre. There was definitely a chance she could win. Possibly only a slim one, but better than no chance at all.

Chapter Twenty-Three

Cassidy eased slowly away from Gabe and slipped out of bed.

"It's too early. Come back to sleep," he muttered, his eyes half open.

"You can go back to sleep, but it's late afternoon. And I'm hungry."

Gabe groaned as he struggled to his feet. "What's wrong with sleeping in?"

Cassidy stared at him. "Sleeping in? Didn't you hear me say late afternoon?"

"Is the sun still up?" When Cassidy nodded, Gabe continued. "Then I repeat, what's wrong with sleeping in?"

She shook her head. "I'm getting something to eat."

"Try ice cream with your cereal. Has to beat eating it dry," Gabe called after her.

She nearly reached the kitchen when the phone

rang. She froze. It continued to ring. She slowly walked back to the lounge room to stare at the phone. The caller ID read private.

"Are you going to answer that?"

Cassidy looked up to see Gabe standing in the doorway wearing his usual black jeans. "Maybe." The phone continued to ring.

Gabe strode into the room and reached for the phone.

"Don't touch it." She hit his hand away.

"So I guess that's a maybe not."

The phone stopped ringing and Cassidy headed for the kitchen. She grabbed out cornflakes and a bowl.

"You answered when I rang."

"That was really late. And you weren't here."

"So if someone wants you to answer the phone they need to ring after midnight." Gabe put the kettle on.

"Is there a point to this conversation?" She glared at him over her bowl of dry cereal.

"Do you have a mobile phone?"

She shrugged. "I don't know."

"How can you not know if you have a mobile phone?" He took a cup from the cupboard and held it up. "You want coffee?"

Cassidy shook her head. "I threw it at my wall

because it wouldn't stop ringing. Now it's under my bed. If you want to know if it still works have a look for yourself." She strode from the room, ignoring Gabe when he called her name. She retreated to her room, locking the door before she slid down it to sit on the floor. She banged her head against the door several times then swore.

She should apologise, but she couldn't bring herself to do it. Her mood had gone to crap the moment she'd woken and realised she knew the ritual off by heart. There was no excuse to postpone hunting Castigate. Other than she was scared to hell of facing him. She set her half eaten bowl of cereal aside and drew up her legs to drop her head onto her knees.

"Cass?"

"What?" She winced at the snap in her voice.

"Can I come in?"

"What for?"

"So you can tell me what's wrong. You've been in a bad mood since you got up this morning."

"Nothing's wrong." She rested her head against the door again.

"Then I guess you must have got out of the wrong side of bed."

"You were on that side."

"I know."

She reluctantly smiled at the humour she could hear in his voice. "I'm still not letting you in."

"Okay. If you don't want to talk to me, is there someone else you'd rather talk to?"

Cassidy was on her feet with the door open and snapping out the word 'no' before she had time to think.

"Whoa. Steady on." Gabe reached for her, pulling her close. "You don't have to speak to anyone at all if you don't want. We'll stand here all afternoon without a word." He remained silent a moment. "Hmm, I couldn't think of anything I'd rather do than hold you all afternoon."

"What happened to the silent part?"

He laughed softly. "I used to get into trouble for talking in class. I don't think the silent part's going to work real well. Maybe you can do the silent part and I'll do the talking part."

"I know the ritual off by heart."

Gabe pulled back to stare down at her for a moment. "Okay, that was a conversation stopper for a minute there. So what are we going to do about it?"

"It feels suicidal to even think about going after Castigate. I don't want to die."

"Let's run away then. I vote for somewhere with a beach. I like to swim. You can pick the next destination. A week tops at each place. That should keep him at bay."

Cassidy groaned, pressing her face to his chest. "We've got to face him. I'm just not sure I can do it tonight."

"Cass." He waited for her to meet his gaze. "Whenever you're ready. You don't have to rush this. I'm not going anywhere"

She reached up to press a finger to his lips, running it down to his chin like he often did to her. She smiled when he bent his head and nipped her finger. "Why are you here?"

"I thought we'd already decided that. I'm crazy, remember?" He moved forward to brush his lips across hers. "Absolutely crazy… about you."

"You've certainly got the crazy part right," she said just before he kissed her again, this time more than a brush of lips. His hand went to the back of her neck, the other staying at her waist. Cassidy tried to remember why it was a bad idea, then she recalled as she felt the day ending and pulled away from him. She stared up at him, lips still parted. "The sun's set."

"You felt it?"

She nodded.

Gabe grinned. "I guess that makes you officially a hunter then."

"Really?"

"It's not just about hunting them down, you've also got to know when they're about and how close to dawn and dusk it is. Not to mention the feel of three a.m. when they're most powerful."

She frowned. "That's what Castigate was planning."

"Huh?"

"He'd expected my father to start the ritual at three and be there at four to catch Remedy. It wasn't about four people at all. It was about the time. Dad stuffed up his plans by being impatient. Whatever happened I bet Castigate wasn't going to let anyone walk away from that building. Not Dad, not Remedy and not me. It was a set up right from the start." She felt anger burn away the fear. Remedy had been right. She wasn't blaming the one who deserved it.

"So what are we going to do about it, demon girl?" Gabe touched her lightly on the face near her left eye.

She smiled, guessing there must be flames in her eyes. "We're going to make sure he regrets ever messing with my family. But first, I have some things to do." When Gabe started to speak she shook her head. "Alone." There were people she needed to see. She wouldn't have got so angry at Gabe's suggestion to talk to someone else if she hadn't already been thinking it was past time she did.

Gabe stared at her a moment before he nodded. "Make sure you take plenty of blades with you. And I've got holy water in my room if your vials need topping up."

Her smile became a grin. "Well that's a change from, have you got your phone and purse?"

"No point giving you your phone until I find out if it works."

She shook her head. "I don't need a phone."

"Humour me. You can ignore all other calls but it'd be nice if you'd answer mine, okay?"

"Fine. But you get it. I'm not climbing under my bed. It's been months since it was cleaned under there."

"The sacrifices I make," Gabe said as he strode to the bed and crouched down to have a look. "I can see it. I think."

She smiled as she watched him, admiring the way the denim fit him. "Take all the time you need." She grinned when he looked back at her. He grinned at her before he returned to rescuing her phone.

Moments later, he held it up triumphantly. "Still looks in one piece. How about I charge it and see how it handled the impact."

"The charger is still plugged into the power point on the other side of my bed." She hadn't seen any point in removing it. There hadn't been a reason to. "But if it's not charged by the time I'm ready to go, I'm not waiting around."

Gabe chuckled. "Not even if I asked you really nicely?" He plugged the phone into the charger before crossing the room to stand in front of her.

"No." But she could see that he didn't believe her. "I'm serious."

"I know." He continued to smile.

"You're not wearing me down."

"So what do you want to do while we wait for the phone to charge?"

She slowly shook her head, a reluctant smile forming. "Practice sword fighting?" After her daggers, it would have to be her favourite form of combat.

"Up close and personal. Sounds good."

She rolled her eyes, pushing past him to stride to his room. But he was right. She much preferred that style of fighting to using ranged weapons.

Chapter Twenty-Four

Cassidy stood in the hallway, staring at the door several metres away. She couldn't bring herself to take the last handful of steps to her mum's doorway. In the past two weeks she'd faced down numerous demons, hunting them and even sending some back to hell. Yet she couldn't cross the distance separating her and her mum. How pathetic was that? Her jaw clenched. This was ridiculous. She couldn't stand here all night. Forcing her feet to carry her to the doorway, she stared in at her mum.

It had been months since she'd seen her. She barely recognised the woman sitting in the chair staring at nothing. Taking another step forward, her hand continued to grip the door frame tightly. Letting go, she started to turn away. She couldn't do this. Hunting demons was far easier.

"Have you brought my dinner?"

Cassidy turned back to face her mum. "Ahh… no."

"That's okay. I'm not very hungry." Sylvia smiled. "I guess I'm just lonely. Tony's taking our little girl for a walk in her pram. He couldn't wait to try it out. Maybe you saw her on the way in here? She's a doll. Not much hair though, but hopefully that'll change."

"Oh?" Cassidy's gaze darted around the room. Nothing gave her inspiration, but it didn't seem to matter. Her mum continued even without further encouragement.

"Eleven hours labour. And for such a tiny little thing. Not even eight pounds. But the most beautiful smile already. That nurse earlier tried to tell me it was wind." Sylvia made a negative motion with her hand. "What would she know?"

Cassidy could only shake her head, her throat filled with a lump almost too difficult to swallow past.

Sylvia giggled. "I wanted to call her Treasure, but Tony wouldn't let me. After all those hours of labour and then having her put in my arms, all I could say was what a little treasure. But Cassidy's a good name. I think she'll like it. What do you think?"

"I… I have to… go." She started to turn away then remembered what her father had asked of her. "D… Tony. He loves you. He wanted me to tell you."

"You did see them on your way in."

Cassidy nodded. "They both love you." She spun and ran from the room, not stopping until she was outside, hands on her knees as she leaned forward, gasping in gulps of hot summer night air. She wanted to throw back her head and scream. Anger and pain burned through her and she wanted to hurt something. Make something else feel the pain instead of being the one to feel it.

She spun to face Remedy as she felt him drop out of the sky to land near her. "What do you want?"

"What's wrong? Where's the danger?"

She stared at him a moment. "There's none."

His eyes narrowed. "I would swear you're telling the truth, but I sensed your pain."

"My mum's in there." She gestured towards the building behind him.

He inclined his head and started to turn away.

"I want you to heal her." It took all her willpower not to beg.

"I'm not some genie who grants wishes."

"But you could heal her, you were going to."

"You didn't honour the bargain made."

"I wasn't about to kill myself."

Remedy held her gaze, flames burning brightly in his eyes. "I can't heal her."

"You lied to us?"

He shook his head. "I'm as bound by my word as a human is bound by rope. More so. Rope can be cut. My word can't."

"What's that supposed to mean?"

"I gave my word to heal her in exchange for yours and your father's deaths."

"Change it. Make another deal."

"It doesn't work like that. Nor can you try and bargain with another demon to cure her. I am bound to prevent them."

She crossed the space between them, grabbing fistfuls of the shirt he'd materialised once his wings had disappeared. "Make it work. I want my mum healed."

"It would kill both of us. Is that what you want? To die? If so, you should have stepped out of the circle the night your father summoned me." He untangled her hands from his shirt, his tone cold.

"No. There has to be another way."

He remained silent.

"Ib–"

"Don't." This time it was him grabbing a fistful of her shirt as he dragged her close. "You agreed not to speak that name. Invoke it and force me to heal your mother and it will kill us. The deal was made, it cannot be unmade. Our life for her health. That's the only way."

She wanted to protest, wanted to tell him he lied. But she could taste the truth of his words. Anger evaporated. "I miss her." The words were soft and she looked away from his gaze, unable to hold it any longer.

He let her go. "Where is the boy?"

"At home."

"Why isn't he with you?"

She raised her chin. "I didn't need him here. I can visit my mum without anyone's help."

"Maybe you shouldn't." He turned, striding away from her.

She wanted to yell at him to come back. That she wasn't finished talking to him. But what else could she say? Nothing could change the situation. Her mum couldn't be healed. Not unless she wanted to give up her life. And even if she was willing, she doubted Remedy would let her.

Her phone rang and for a moment the unfamiliar sound startled her. She pulled it from her pocket and stared down at it. She glanced around the dark car park. Was Gabe following her? She put the phone to her ear as she pressed the connection button. "Yes?"

Her voice was low and hesitant. Why was he ringing?

"I wanted to let you know I'm not at home. I got a lift to a gym. It was boring at home without you."

"Okay." How was it that he always managed to be there when she needed him, even if it was only a phone call?

"Think you can pick me up once you've finished your mysterious errands?"

"Where are you?" She repeated back the address he gave her.

"Are you okay?"

She remained silent a moment. "Yeah."

"You can pick me up now if you need some company."

She thought about it, but finally said, "No." There was one more thing she had to do on her own. Hopefully it wouldn't be as difficult as visiting her mum had been.

"See you later then."

"Yeah." She stared at the phone for a minute once she'd disconnected. What was he, psychic? She shook her head. Obviously he had good timing. Sometimes. She tucked her phone in her pocket and took a deep breath. The pain was subsiding. Striding to her motorbike, she tried not to think about the next destination. Once she reached it, she stilled, checking the area for demons. She was still safe. The direction she was headed in only had minor ones. They wouldn't be a problem. The moment they felt her come into their area they'd probably head as far from her as possible.

Twenty minutes later she pulled up in front of a highset house. She hung her helmet from the handlebars and strode around the back, slipping through the wooden gate that had a broken hinge and always sat partly open. She stopped in front of a tree that branched out towards the house and picked the corner of her scab, smearing only a little blood across her mark. Energy rushed through her, not as much as when she used it to fight, but she didn't need that much.

Jumping for the first branch she swung herself up, making her way towards Amy's window where she was bent over a laptop at her desk. She was probably messaging her numerous friends. She'd always been the more outgoing of the two of them. Reaching the window, Cassidy popped the screen out and dropped silently onto the carpet.

Amy turned at her movement, and eyes wide, her mouth gaped open. Worried she'd scream Cassidy was across the room in a flash, hand pressed to Amy's mouth. "Shh. It's me."

Chapter Twenty-Five

Amy pulled her hand away. "What the hell have you done to yourself?" She reached out and gingerly touched Cassidy's jagged hair. "And a tattoo? I thought we were going to get butterflies together." She gestured towards the demon mark that had grown a few centimetres since Cassidy had acquired it. "And why haven't you answered any of my phone calls, texts, emails and letters?" Amy swore as she wiped at her eyes. "And how dare you make me cry. It makes my eyes all puffy." She threw her arms around Cassidy.

"You're choking me." Cassidy tried to loosen the grip around her neck, not quite sure how to react. She wasn't the same person Amy had befriended years ago.

"Serves you right." Amy pulled away to glare at her. "We're meant to be best friends." One hand went to her hip as her green eyes narrowed. The other hand became an accusing finger. "You don't just drop off the face of the earth. I didn't care if you didn't want to talk. I just wanted to be there with you. I still do."

"Sorry."

"Damn it." Amy threw her arms around Cassidy again. "Don't you dare disappear on me again."

Cassidy smiled as she brushed the wavy brown hair away from her face. "I missed you."

"So you should. I even considered breaking into your house. Smashing a window or something."

"I needed time alone." Cassidy pulled away when Amy's grip loosened.

"I went to the funeral hoping to see you."

Cassidy shrugged, her gaze going to a point past Amy's shoulder. "I couldn't go." She hoped Amy wasn't going to expect her to talk about it, because she really couldn't.

"Cass–"

"I can't stay." She caught Amy's hands before she could hug her again. "I just wanted to see you. For a few minutes."

Amy's gaze roamed her face. "What's wrong? And you've lost too much weight. You need to eat lots of chocolate. Maybe some ice cream too. Or get a tub of chocolate ice cream."

"Amy, quiet for a minute." They both fell silent and Cassidy stared at her friend, glad that at least she was still the same. "Give me more time. Okay? I'll call you when I'm ready to talk."

"If it takes longer than a couple of weeks I'm going to start sending daily emails again."

"Daily?"

Amy threw her hands up in the air. "Great. All that effort wasted. You haven't even seen them."

Cassidy's lips slowly curved into a smile. "I will. But not yet. I just wanted to see you for a few minutes." She hadn't wanted to face Castigate without having had a chance to say goodbye, just in case. She backed away towards the window. "I'll call you one day soon." She hoped. If everything went according to plan. Well, that was if she ever came up with a plan.

"You know you can go out the front door. You don't have to go all ninja on me just because you're wearing black. You used to love bright colours. And what's with the motorbike boots?"

"Question one, no I can't. Question two, people change and question three, they go with my motorbike."

Amy's mouth rounded and for a moment she was quiet. "What sort of bike? And when did you get a license? And why can't you go out the front door?" She hurried forward, grabbing Cassidy's hands. "And you can't go. I have a million things to tell you. And a trillion to ask."

Cassidy pulled away again, sitting on the window ledge. "Ask me them another day." She hesitated. "Look out for yourself, okay?"

"You too."

Cassidy swung out and grabbed the closest branch, grinning at the gasp behind her. She turned her head to see Amy had both hands covering her mouth. A few seconds later and she was at the base of the tree, giving Amy a quick wave before she headed to her motorbike at the front of the house.

As she swung her leg over the motorbike, the front door burst open. Amy stood there, her arms wrapped around herself. Cassidy pulled on her helmet, started the engine and gave her friend another wave before she took off. Guilt hit her as she glanced once more in her friend's direction before she turned the corner. Amy was still standing out the front of her house, her arms wrapped around her waist. She hadn't been able to stay any longer. After she dealt with Castigate she'd come back and see Amy. That would have to be enough for now.

It didn't take long to arrive at the gym. She sat on her motorbike, helmet on the handlebars as she tilted her head back to look at the stars. At least the second visit hadn't been as bad as the first. She was relieved they were over. Now no matter what happened, she'd said her goodbyes to everyone important in her past. Those who were still living. About to swing her leg over the seat, she stopped when the front door opened. Gabe strode towards her.

"How'd you know I was here?" she asked when he reached her side.

"How do you think, demon girl?" He turned her wrist to show the blood smear. "Any other secret errands to run tonight?"

She shook her head, glad he didn't seem to want to ask questions about where she'd been.

"Does that mean we're going home now?"

Cassidy opened her mouth to answer, but a scream rang out through the night, drawing her attention. She searched the area for demons, using all her senses. She frowned. "I can't find any demons."

"Sometimes they're earthly ones." Gabe started to stride towards the direction the scream had come from.

Cassidy hurried after him. "What are you doing?"

"Checking."

"But if it isn't demons–"

"You going to ignore someone who's in danger?" He shot her a glance.

Cassidy sighed. "I guess not."

"Try not to use weapons. And don't kill anybody."

"What if they've got weapons? And I don't plan on killing anyone. Why would you even say that?"

Gabe grabbed her left arm and held it up. "Because you're stronger than humans and you're used to fighting demons. If they've got a weapon get it off them and use that. But don't leave it behind. The last thing you need is the cops running your prints. And no blood either."

"Because of DNA?"

"Nope. Because of demons." He grinned at her as they entered a well treed park.

Cassidy looked around, her gaze zeroing in on the drama. Two men held a struggling girl, one of them with his hand across her mouth. Another three men took turns at holding and hitting a boy that looked seventeen, his muscular build no match for their numbers. The girl appeared to be the same age as the boy. "You get the girl." Cassidy sprinted towards the people.

Gabe ran beside her. "Why do you get the extra one to fight?"

"If you finish with your two before me, I'll share." She shot him a quick grin then threw herself into the fight, blocking a punched aimed at the boy. She drove her fist into the man's stomach and winced when he hit the ground. She had no time to check how badly she'd hurt him. The other two threw themselves at her, dropping the boy to the ground, where he remained curled up. Throwing a fist at one, she spun and blocked a hit from the other, quickly following that with a punch to his jaw. There was a crack when her fist connected and he collapsed in front of her. She spun back to face the other man, only to find him sprawled, unconscious on the ground. She hadn't thought she'd hit him that hard.

"Shut up, just everyone shut up," a man called from behind her.

At the same time, Gabe warned, "He's got a gun."

Cassidy spun, taking in the scene. One of the men who'd been fighting Gabe was on the ground while the other waved a handgun in the air. Gabe backed away and the girl sobbed on the ground. Cassidy's gaze was drawn back to Gabe. Relief rushed through her when she saw he was fine.

"Shut up. Do you hear me? Shut up." The man pointed the gun at the sobbing girl.

Cassidy's eyes narrowed and she raked her nails over her demon mark, breaking open the cut and smearing blood across her wrist. She fought the urge to throw back her head and laugh at the power that filled her, heightening all her senses. "I think I broke your mate's jaw. Maybe you should worry about getting him to a hospital instead of waving that gun around." She stalked towards him, hands at her side.

The gun swung towards Cassidy. "Back off. Not another step or I'll kill you."

"I think we need Remedy," Gabe called. The gun swung towards him.

"No we don't I've got this all under control. But a shuriken would be appreciated." Cassidy continued her steady pace forward.

"Enough!" The man swung the gun wildly between Cassidy, Gabe and the girl.

The moment the gunman's gaze wasn't on her, Cassidy pointed at Gabe, then the gunman and then tapped her right wrist. She mimed throwing a blade. Gabe shook his head. She didn't even have time to argue in any way before the gunman was looking at her again. "Drop the gun and walk away. Don't do anything you'll regret." She could tell him all about regrets.

"Please. Please." The girl's sobs grew louder.

"I said shut up!" The man turned the gun on the girl again.

The world slowed down for Cassidy. She saw him pull the trigger. She didn't have time to blink before she was carrying the girl from the path of the bullet. She felt wood splinter beside her as she dropped the girl on the ground under another tree, spinning to face the man. She was in time to see a small blade strike his wrist and the gun fall to the ground. His uninjured hand rose, his mouth opened and he screamed, pointing at Cassidy, eyes wide. In the background she heard the sound of sirens as she continued towards the man.

"We've got to get out of here." Gabe ran towards her.

Cassidy pulled the blade from the man who backed away from her, begging her not to hurt him. She grinned at him and leaned into his face. "Boo."

He yelped, stumbled and landed on the ground, staring up at her. "Please, please. Stay away. Whatever you are, just stay away from me. Please. The fire. Take it away from me." He slowly scooted back across the ground.

Gabe grabbed Cassidy's right wrist and tugged her away. "Come on. Do you really want to talk to the cops?"

The world started to catch up to normal pace and she turned to Gabe with a shake of her head. She ran with him to her motorbike, pulling on her helmet as she hopped on. The moment she felt Gabe seated behind her she took off, heading in the opposite direction to the sound of sirens. After a few minutes she changed directions and headed for home.

Chapter Twenty-Six

When they arrived home energy still sang through Cassidy's body, making her restless. She turned to Gabe the moment they stepped inside and held out the blade to him. "I thought I asked for a shuriken."

"I told you no weapons."

"He had a gun. Besides, it's a stupid rule."

"No, it's not. We don't use weapons against humans in case someone is recording the fight. Everyone records things these days. The last thing we need is to end up on YouTube."

Cassidy grinned. "And how would they explain a YouTube vid of a hunter fighting a demon? Or even empty air if the demon's hidden."

"Cameras are better at picking up such things. And it doesn't matter because people would think they'd recorded actors."

Cassidy shrugged. "He had a gun. I wasn't about to stand around and wait to be shot."

"You're lucky I had time to throw anything. What were you even thinking? Were you trying to get yourself killed? You're not a demon." His hands went to her shoulders, shaking her lightly as his grip tightened. "Damn it. He could have killed you."

"He didn't." She dropped the blade Gabe ignored and lifted her hands to push his away. "I have never felt so much energy. He had no chance of hitting me."

Gabe raised her left arm. "That's because it wasn't just your blood feeding the demon tonight. Judging by all those splatters on your arm I'd say you broke a nose as well as a jaw."

Cassidy took a step back. "That's a stranger's blood on my arm?" At Gabe's nod she paled and ran to the bathroom. She heard Gabe enter the room after she'd scrubbed most of the blood off. "That's disgusting." She turned on Gabe with a glare when he laughed.

"Glad to see you're not as demonic as you looked earlier."

"What's that supposed to mean?"

Gabe stepped close. "Your eyes were all flame. They're not much better right now. And look at your mark."

Cassidy didn't have to look at it to feel how it twisted and turned. "Fire." She repeated the gunman's word.

"Yeah." Gabe nodded as he brushed the side of her face near her left eye. "Fire."

Cassidy closed her eyes, trying to contain the power. It was impossible. She opened her eyes to stare at Gabe. "I need to hunt."

"Need?"

She nodded. "I feel like someone's hooked me up to the electricity grid."

Gabe's lips slowly curved into a smile. "I can think of a better way to wear off all that energy." The smile became a grin. "But hunting's probably the safest option."

Cassidy laughed as she shook her head. "You coming with me?"

Gabe wrapped an arm around her waist and pulled her close, his lips a breath away. "Always." He pulled back slightly. "Now let's get out of here before I get myself killed." He brushed a finger across her lips before he turned away, reaching out to take her hand and tug her along with him.

Once they were on the motorbike, Cassidy searched for demons. She could sense Castigate off to the north. Obviously not a direction they should be going in. She quickly searched in a different direction. They were too minor. Then she found one.

Grinning, she headed towards him. It took them nearly half an hour to track him down. She reached for her daggers as soon as she was off the motorbike.

Gabe put a hand on her arm. "He's not doing anything yet."

She shook Gabe's hand off her. "But he will be. Why else is he following that couple along the footpath?"

"Guarding them?"

"Yeah, right."

"When he does something wrong then we can step in."

"It's a stupid rule." The energy raced through her, looking for an outlet. And the one she'd chosen was continuing to walk away from her.

"Without rules you might as well be a demon."

She stopped walking to face him, growling between gritted teeth. "I'm not a demon."

Gabe raised his left hand. "Aren't you? Then why do you feel exactly like one right now?"

He was wrong. "I need to hunt. And you're stopping me." There was already too much energy racing through her, but the only thing she could think of to catch the other demon's attention was to increase it. Running her fingernails across her wrist, she grinned. "Guess I'll have to do something about it."

Swearing, he reached out to grab her right hand, but he was too slow. "One day you'll call up more energy than your body can handle." He spun to face the demon that came towards them.

"They're mine. I saw them first. Go find your own humans."

Gabe took out two of his blades. "We're here to protect them."

The demon laughed. "A hunter and a demon together?" He turned his gaze on Cassidy. "Leave behind that pretty shell you wear and come hunt with me. If this hunter has bound you I'll get rid of him for you." His grin showed pointed teeth. "I haven't had the pleasure of killing a hunter in years."

"Is that enough proof for you?" Cassidy asked Gabe. Her gaze remained on the demon, her daggers ready.

"You admit to killing a hunter?" Gabe asked.

The demon chuckled. "What are you going to do about it, boy?"

"I don't know what he's going to do about it, but I plan to do plenty." Grinning, Cassidy leapt at the demon, slashing at him with her daggers.

He spun away, but not before she'd managed to cut him. Roaring, he attacked her with a sword he materialised. She darted past his blade, coming up behind him to strike at his back before she whirled away from him.

"I offered to set you free." The demon blocked the blades Gabe threw at him, moving to put Cassidy between him and Gabe.

"I'm not a demon." She struck out at him, trying to get out of Gabe's way.

The demon didn't cooperate, continuing to keep her between him and Gabe. "Then what are you?"

She hadn't liked the word the first time she'd heard it. But now it meant power. It also meant not cowering before a demon who could take her life or the life of those she loved. Her lips curved into a smile as she renewed her attacks, the power singing through her. "Tainted." She could feel other demons in the distance, picking up on the power and heading towards them.

"You were a hunter?" The demon continued to block her attacks, still keeping her between him and Gabe.

"No. I was, and still am, human." She could feel her humanity beneath the demon power and she didn't plan to lose it.

"With eyes like that? Not likely."

"Stop playing with him, demon girl. Can't you feel the others?" Gabe demanded, trying to move to his right.

Yeah, she could feel them. And she looked forward to it. A glance in the direction the two humans had been walking showed they were long gone. Dropping her daggers, she laughed as the power surged through her. She vaulted over the demon, a hand on his shoulder to push herself over. Grabbing his arm, she twisted it up behind his back, struggling to hold him. "Turn him into a pincushion."

Gabe launched blade after blade at the struggling demon until he burst into flames, howling as he returned to hell. As soon as the demon was gone, Gabe began to gather up his blades. "They're coming in fast. Are we staying or going?"

Picking up her daggers, she searched the area, power still singing through her body. There was nothing strong coming for them. Only the minor. But there should be enough of them to make it challenging. "We stay."

Gabe laughed, dropping an arm around her shoulders as they faced the direction the first wave of demons would come from. "I should have known. Especially with how much power is still pouring off you. Remember you're meant to be using it up, not adding to it."

"Are you tired? Having trouble keeping up?"

"Not at all." His lips met hers for a moment, then he stared down at her. "Hunting is my second favourite pastime."

She grinned at him, not bothering to ask what his favourite was. With that expression, she didn't need to. "Then why are we waiting for them?" Shrugging his arm off her shoulders, she raced forward, meeting up with the first demon halfway down the street.

By the time the next few arrived, they'd dispatched the first one. The next two were starved for power. She could feel their hunger for hers. She wasn't about to give it up. It had been too hard won.

Her daggers streaked through the night, a blur of motion as she attacked and blocked, trying to keep out of Gabe's way as he threw his blades. At one stage of the night, he ran out and Cassidy drew the demons away from him so he had a chance to collect his weapons.

As dawn arrived, Cassidy sank her dagger into the demon she had pinned to the ground, a weary smile forming as it disappeared in a mist that hung on the air for a few seconds. She looked up at Gabe who held out a hand to her. Taking it, she rose to her feet.

"Ready to go home?"

She nodded. "Now I am." Her smile widened. "How about you?"

Chuckling, he slung his arm around her shoulders. "More than, demon girl." He walked beside her towards her motorbike. "You want to be passenger this time?"

"Not likely." She swung her leg over the motorbike, pulling on her helmet. Searching the area she found that even Castigate was gone. And the few minor demons that were able to roam during daylight hours were nowhere near them. Once Gabe was behind her, she headed for home. It had been a good night's work. Hopefully tonight would be just as easy. But she doubted it. She couldn't stop thinking about how much power Castigate had. She wasn't about to let that keep her from going after him. She owed him for what he'd done to her family.

Chapter Twenty-Seven

Cassidy lay beside Gabe, staring at the ceiling as she listened to him breathing. She rubbed her thumb over the ring, feeling it turn slightly. Tonight. It would have to be tonight before she chickened out. If she left it too long she might come up with excuses of why she shouldn't go after him. There were certainly plenty of them to choose from. The one that came to mind first was that he was far stronger than her.

Gabe rolled towards her, pulling her close. "Do you have to think so loud? I was trying to sleep."

"I'm going after Castigate tonight."

"I know."

"Yeah, right."

Gabe smiled at her. "We're going after Castigate tonight."

She pulled away from him so she could sit up. "You

don't have to come and how can you say you know. Are you a mind reader now?"

Gabe rolled onto his back, still smiling. "No, but I'm starting to be able to read you. All your sighs and restlessness just now. And who were you saying goodbye to last night?"

"None of your business." She slid across the bed and swung her feet over the edge. "And who says I was saying goodbye to anyone?"

"I rang my family and talked to them last night. Then Riley took me to see our priest before he dropped me off at the gym."

She couldn't risk him. There was no way she was going to let anyone else she cared about die. "I've changed my mind. I don't need help." She rose to her feet, backing away from the bed.

Gabe hopped out of bed following her until she stopped near the door. "We're not going to lose. I've got an idea."

"It's not one of your religious fanatic ideas, is it?"

"No. Just one of the few family rules I haven't got around to breaking before." He grinned. "I knew you were going to be a bad influence on me." He took another step closer.

Cassidy held up a hand, pressing against his chest to prevent him from coming any closer. "I thought all your family rules were important to you lot and to do with the way you fight demons."

"Some things are more important than others." He stepped to the side, brushing her arm out of the way so he could close the gap between them. "I've been thinking about what you told me about the night you and Remedy became inseparable. There's no easy way to break the bond between you, not without a really high chance you'll die. You did a good job of that binding. So we have to deal with Castigate before he destroys Remedy." His hands slid across her back. "I don't want you to die."

"I don't want you to die either."

"Good. We agree on something. So come on, off to the kitchen."

Cassidy frowned as Gabe led her to the kitchen, tugging on her hand when she slowed. "No matter how many times I replay your comment it still isn't a logical conclusion to that conversation."

Gabe glanced towards her with a fleeting grin as he stopped at the kitchen sink. Letting go of her hand, he picked up his blade that lay on the stainless steel sink, beside the clean dishes in the draining rack. "Grab out the cling wrap for me."

Cassidy pulled the roll of cling wrap from a drawer

and gasped when she turned to see Gabe run the blade lightly across his arm. "What are you doing?"

"Tear me off a piece of that, will you?"

Cassidy handed him a length of cling wrap and watched as he smeared it with blood before wrapping it in on itself. "What am I meant to do with this?" She stared at the bloody cling wrap he handed her.

"Put it in the fridge until we hunt. Wrap it around your wrist when you need an extra boost. But I'd really prefer you didn't use it when I'm occupied since it's going to be painful for me."

"You're giving me your blood to use?" Cassidy stared up at him. When he nodded, she threw her arms about him. "That's the nicest thing anyone's ever done for me."

"In that case you've definitely been hanging with the wrong people. I'd say a single rose would have to be nicer. This is practical."

"I know what your blood means to you. Don't joke about what you're doing. Thank you." She rose on tiptoes to press her lips against his. Warmth spiralled through her as her arms tightened around him.

It was Gabe who ended things this time. He pulled back, a slight smile as he stared down at her. "As much as I'd like to continue this, I think we should prepare for a visitor."

"I need to see him. I've got something to ask him." She headed for the fridge, putting the bloody cling wrap in the shelf at the top of the door. She stared at it a moment longer before she closed it to turn and meet Gabe's eyes. "Do you really think we've got a chance?"

He held her gaze steadily. "Yes."

"This is nice to see. Some distance between the two of you for a change." Remedy strolled into the kitchen.

Gabe grinned. "I know. It surprises the hell out of me too."

Remedy pointed a finger at him. "Don't start, boy." He turned to Cassidy. "Why did you want me?"

"I didn't call you." She frowned. "At least I don't think so."

"You've been tugging at me for the past few minutes since the sun set. So again, why did you want me?"

Well that was handy to know. She'd only been trying to figure out where he was. "I need you to teach me how to fight. Without weapons."

"And what will you give me in exchange?"

"I didn't have to give you anything last time."

"And see what happens? Now you expect to make more demands on me and have them met." Remedy shook his head. "Nothing comes without a price for a reason. I am not your slave to be at your beck and call. Now what will you give me in exchange?"

Cassidy stared at Remedy, then her gaze dropped to her demon mark before falling on Gabe who hadn't moved position. She was going to do it anyway, so why not call it a payment. She rubbed at her wrist, feeling the scab beneath her palm, wondering if it would ever have a chance to heal. As she watched him, Gabe ran a finger across the cut he'd made earlier, his brows raised. Cassidy nodded. Gabe stared at her a moment longer before he slowly nodded, his lips curving into a grin.

Chapter Twenty-Eight

Cassidy turned back to Remedy who had quietly watched the exchange. "I will give you some of his blood before sunrise."

"You will offer me blood from the hunter. Why would he agree to this?" Remedy looked between each of them. "Hunters never give their blood to demons."

"I'm not giving you my blood," Gabe said. His gaze returned to Cassidy. "I'm giving it to Cass. It's her choice what she does with it."

"How much blood are we talking and how do you plan to give it to me?"

Cassidy touched her demon mark again. "Through me."

"Will it be more than that pathetic little splash of new blood you gave me last night?"

Cassidy nodded. "Yes."

"More than the smear you stole from the boy last time?"

"Yes." Again Cassidy nodded.

"You're going after Castigate tonight, aren't you?"

What else could she say? He would hear any lie she spoke. "Yes."

Remedy crossed the short distance between them, stopping right in front of her. "You cannot call me. Castigate would have control of me, of us, within seconds of me arriving. No matter how you pull and tug at me or what you say, I will not join you."

"Actually, if you called him by his true name he'd have to come. Immediately," Gabe said.

Remedy turned his gaze on Gabe. "Silence, or I will silence you."

Gabe strolled across the kitchen to stand toe to toe with Remedy. "She needs to know. Without the correct information she could make a mistake. Would you prefer she accidentally called you?"

"I would prefer she flee with me. Although I can say we are the same power, there are minor differences. After all this time he has known my name, he is the stronger one. It takes very little to tip the scales in battle." Remedy turned to Cassidy. "We can bring your boy. I will let you have him if you agree to leave this very minute and each time I say we must move to another place."

"Run for eternity?" Cassidy shook her head. "Not going to happen. Now do we have a deal? Blood for knowledge."

Remedy stared at her, flames flickering in the depths of his eyes. He gave a sharp nod then reached for her face. Even though she was prepared, the bombardment still hit her like a physical blow. Image after image, as she learned how to move in a fight. Centuries of knowledge crammed into her in the space of minutes. Then she was released and she leaned gasping against the door of the fridge.

Gabe handed her a glass of water and she shakily wrapped a hand around it to bring it to her lips. The cool liquid helped centre her body and she stopped feeling like it belonged to someone else. She smiled slightly at Gabe before she turned to Remedy. "Thank you."

Remedy shook his head. "I have done you no favour. If you reach the point where you have no weapons but your own limbs then you might as well give up."

"You should know I don't give up." Cassidy grinned. "Ever."

Remedy nodded. "You do surprise me at times."

He lifted her right hand to look at the gold ring. His gaze returned to hers. "If you manage to do this, never lose the ring. He will still know my true name and that can be used against us in the wrong hands."

"Okay."

"Call me when it is done." Remedy spun on his heels and strode from the kitchen.

Cassidy watched him go before she turned to Gabe. "How can we stop Castigate from leaving an area?"

Gabe shrugged. "A circle of power I guess."

"Salt?"

He nodded. "It works the same way as when you keep them out. They can't cross over whether they're on the inside or outside. What are you thinking?"

"I don't know." She frowned. "How much power will your blood give me?"

"Not as much as it would give you if you were a true demon. Or even if you accepted a demon inside you."

"Inside?" She stared at Gabe, waiting for an explanation.

"Like he was wearing your skin. Feeding you his power, helping control your body, and if you're very unlucky taking it over completely." His lips twisted into a smile. "Most people are unlucky when it comes to demons." He hesitated. "Are you really sure you want to do this? You don't want to take Remedy's offer?"

"To kidnap you and run?"

Gabe chuckled. "I can't say I like the kidnap part." He lowered his voice. "But he did say you could have me. Now I'm all for that part of the plan."

Cassidy tried to hold back her smile, but it was impossible. She reached out and drew him to her, resting her head against him. "You don't have to stay."

"I know. I choose to stay."

"Why?" She lifted her head to stare at him.

"Someone has to stick around and cook you breakfast. Dry cereal can't be too appetising."

She hit his chest. "Why?"

"Idiot. Why the hell do you think?" His lips met hers and questions were forgotten as bodies pressed close and hands slid over skin. He finally pulled back to stare down at her, a hand pressed against her back, her shirt bunched over it. "Don't you dare take on Castigate unless you're sure you have a chance of winning."

Cassidy stared at him, lips slightly parted. She eventually nodded. "Are you sure you want to come with me? I don't want anything to happen to you."

"Then I guess we'll just have to look out for each other. Now what's the plan?"

"To see sunrise?"

Gabe laughed. "Sounds good to me. So how are we going to go about that?"

"Really good question. I'll tell you when I know all the details."

"Okay, flying by the seat of your pants. Not a perfect plan, but at least we've got one."

Cassidy returned his grin. "Yeah. Better than none at all."

Gabe laughed again, this time throwing his head back and spinning her around the kitchen. "Bring it on. I love a challenging hunt."

"Then let's go arm ourselves."

Lowering her to her feet, Gabe shook his head. "Breakfast first. Something more filling than dry cereal."

She slowly drew away, reluctant to break contact with him. "You make breakfast and I'll shower and start getting ready." She wanted to take more than just her daggers with her. An entire arsenal might be enough. If they needed more than that, then Remedy was probably right. If it got down to hand to hand combat there was a good chance they were going to lose.

"Need someone to scrub your back?"

She laughed, glad he'd drawn her away from her depressing thoughts. "Then who would cook breakfast?" Turning, she left the room, the sound of his laughter following her to the bathroom.

Chapter Twenty-Nine

Cassidy met Gabe's gaze as she helped him hide the salt circle they hadn't quite completed. She dusted the leaf litter from her hands. "Are you sure this'll work?"

Gabe nodded. "As long as you bring him in from the correct side. We don't want him realising it's here. Then I can close the circle with the rest of the salt. Can you feel him coming yet?"

She shook her head. "I keep tugging at him like I'm hunting him, but maybe he knows I'm not really trying."

"A pity you don't know his true name. Demon's can't ignore that call."

"What if he doesn't come?" Cassidy slipped the tips of her fingers into her pocket to check that Gabe's blood was still there. Although she didn't really need to touch it to know it was. She could smell the blood and it made her demon mark writhe in anticipation.

"Then we try again tomorrow night."

She didn't think she could do this two nights in a row. The waiting was killing her. "I might have decided to run by then."

Gabe smiled. "Where are we going to first? A beach?"

Cassidy started to open her mouth to answer when she felt Castigate move towards them. She clasped her hands together in front of her chest. "I think he's coming." Her voice was soft. Yes, he was definitely headed their way. She tugged on his signature once more, wanting to make sure he knew they were looking for him.

"Are you ready?"

Cassidy mentally catalogued her weapons. Daggers in her boots, sword on her back, a leather case on her right arm with several blades and a bow with a quiver of arrows hidden in a tree nearby. Several vials of holy water were tucked into various pockets, the blood was in a pocket nowhere near the holy water and the ring was on her finger. "I hope so."

"You'll do fine. How far away is he?"

Cassidy stilled as she tugged at his signature. She waved Gabe away. "Hide. Quick. He's moving faster than I expected." She strode forward, not wanting to start in the circle and have him check out the surroundings too carefully. And then he was before her, crackling with power. She drew her sword, wanting more distance between them than the daggers gave her.

Castigate laughed. "You think you can fight me? If I had realised this is what you wanted I would have been here sooner. I can't wait to kill you." He brought his hands together and a sword formed in them. He advanced on her.

Cassidy retreated, watching Castigate warily. She was nearly at the salt circle. He needed to follow her just a little further. Why didn't he rush at her or something?

He stopped advancing. "Where is your master?"

"Not here."

"If you call him I won't kill you slowly. I'll make it quick and painless."

Cassidy retreated some more. Castigate continued to stand still. "I'm not about to call him. I'm going to be too busy killing you."

"Come and try, girl."

"Why don't you see if you can get me first?"

Castigate laughed. He raised his hand and a breeze rushed through the clearing, chasing leaf litter away to reveal the salt circle. "I am not an idiot. Don't treat me like one. It annoys me and people tend to get hurt when I'm annoyed. Call the boy out too."

"No."

"Call him out or I'll tear him apart if I have to drag him from his hiding place."

Gabe strode out from amongst a clump of trees. He held a bow in one hand and there was a quiver on his back. "No need. I'm here."

Castigate looked from one to the other. "What did you think you were going to do? The circle would not hold me forever."

Cassidy shrugged. "It was worth a shot." She continued to hold her sword ready.

"Come face me, little girl. Unless you wish me to start with the boy." Castigate glanced towards Gabe.

Cassidy shook her head. "Leave him be." She slowly walked forward. She had barely cleared the edge of the circle when Castigate attacked. The sound of swords clashing rang out in the night air. Arrows came flying towards her, sinking into Castigate. But even after all their planning, they weren't prepared.

Castigate had her on the ground within minutes, the sword pressed against her heart. "Call him. Use his true name and call him here."

"You call him." Cassidy stared up at Castigate.

There was no way she was going to do his bidding when he would kill her anyway.

"He can't," Gabe called out. "He can't summon him with the name, only use it against him when he's near. Only a human can summon."

"I can't summon him," Cassidy said. "He'd kill me."

Castigate pressed a little harder against her chest. "I will kill you."

"Then what's it matter? I'm dead either way." Cassidy met Castigate's gaze. "Go ahead. Kill me."

"No." The word was torn from Gabe. He ran towards them, stopping just out of arm's reach. "Give me his name. I'll call him. Don't give in like this, Cass."

She couldn't let Gabe call him. That'd be a death sentence for him. "Let me up. I'll do it." Cassidy turned her gaze on Gabe. What was he thinking? If Castigate killed Remedy, she was dead. "You're to stay out of this." She rose to her feet the moment the sword no longer held her down, facing Castigate. "He'll leave the moment he arrives. He'll see you standing here. Calling him won't help you."

"Not if he's wearing my skin," Gabe said.

"No." It was Cassidy's turn to cry out. She crossed the space between them, grabbing hold of his arm.

"No, Gabe. Don't even think it." Hadn't he warned her about the dangers of letting a demon in?

Gabe looked past her to Castigate. "If we do this, you will set us free and not harm us in any way. You may wear my skin and Cassidy will call him."

"It won't help," Cassidy said.

Gabe continued to stare at Castigate who finally nodded. "Then give me a moment with Cassidy. I can convince her."

Cassidy shook her head, letting go of him and taking a step away. Gabe followed her. "No. You're crazy. Insane. We're going to die."

Gabe wrapped his arms around her. "We're not going to die. You will do this. Look around you."

Cassidy did, finding they were in front of the salt circle opening. She frowned. What was he trying to tell her? "Gabe?"

"How can you want to leave this world behind? Don't give up."

"This will kill us. Both of us." Why couldn't Gabe understand? He should run. There was no way she could walk away from this, but he could.

"You will need strength for what you have to do. You will manage." He pressed his fingers against the pocket with his blood. "Your strength sometimes humbles me. Knocks me right off my feet." He touched her face lightly beside her left eye. His other hand tucked the small bag of salt into her back pocket. "Complete this."

Cassidy nodded, staring up at him. Hoping she had understood his message. When he started to pull away, she drew him back to her and threw her arms around him, holding him close. Then their lips met and power crackled around them as Cassidy fought not to run, dragging Gabe with her. Beneath her skin she felt the demon mark twist and turn as if it too might break free and flee. She pulled back from Gabe, her hands cupping his face. "Don't you dare leave me."

Gabe grinned. "We've got a date tomorrow night." Pulling away he took another step closer to the incomplete circle. He met Castigate's gaze squarely. "You may now use me to hide."

Castigate turned to Cassidy. "You agree to this?"

"You can wear Gabe's skin and I will call Remedy. In return you may not harm either of us in any way."

Castigate stared at her a moment longer. "The non harming will last for a year and a day. No longer. After that if either of you seek me out it will be your last action."

"A year and a day." Cassidy nodded in agreement. Hopefully his promise would make it easier for her.

Castigate strode towards Gabe and stood in front of him. Then he seemed to step into him so that only Gabe stood there. "Call." The voice that came from Gabe's mouth was strained.

Cassidy nodded sharply, stepping closer to Gabe. She took a deep breath and turned her back on him, dropping her sword. "Ibaelcaurzanon, come here now." She felt power crackle in the night air and Remedy formed in front of her. She pulled the bloody cling wrap from her pocket, unwrapping it.

"How does it feel to be betrayed again?" Gabe spoke from behind her in the strained voice of earlier.

Remedy roared, Cassidy pressed the blood to her demon mark and behind her Gabe screamed as power rushed through her and Remedy. She rubbed the cling wrap over her wrist, trying to get every last drop. Some of it smeared across her hand. Letting the cling wrap fall to the ground, she spun, pushing Gabe back into the circle. When he landed on the ground, she hurriedly completed the circle with salt. There were now two bodies on the ground, only Castigate was moving as he struggled to get to his feet.

"Get out of here," Cassidy yelled at Remedy. "Now."

"You have much explaining to do." Remedy

pointed an accusing finger at her before he disappeared.

Castigate was on his feet when Cassidy turned back to face him. "You lied to me."

Cassidy shook her head. "No. I called him. Gabe let you wear his skin. That was all we agreed to do."

"I will kill you." His voice was low and threatening.

"You can't." Cassidy wanted to enter the circle and check on Gabe, who lay motionless on the ground. But she couldn't risk it. Not yet.

"In a year and a day I will hunt both of you down and kill you. And I will take days doing it. Each of you will beg to die before I finish with you. Your cries will be music that I will enjoy listening to over and over again."

Cassidy's lips slowly curved into a smile of triumph. He couldn't harm them. But there was nothing stopping her from harming him. She pulled a dagger from her boot and ran it across her right hand before removing the ring and holding it tightly in her bloodstained hand. She crossed the barrier, feeling like she was pushing through heavy air.

"You would not be in here with me if you hadn't tricked me," Castigate said. "Gloat while you can. It will be short lived."

"I don't think so." She strode up to him, her smile becoming a grin. "I think life's about to suck really badly for you." She struck out at him with her dagger, drawing blood on his lower arm. She dropped the dagger and grabbed hold of him before he could realise what she did. The ring was pressed between them and she wrapped her other arm around his arm, holding the hand with the ring tightly in place.

Castigate roared and tried to pry her from him. "You will not do this. Do you hear me? Stop now."

Cassidy ignored him, reciting the words she'd learned off by heart, struggling to hold onto him. He twisted and turned, but she clung to him as she spoke the words to bind him. Then Gabe was at her side, helping her hold on. As she reached the last line of the ritual, her gaze met Castigate's. "Forever bound to this ring I hold between us, in service to the one who holds it."

Power filled the air and Cassidy felt like she was struck by lightning. She was flung back to the far edge of the circle. Castigate disappeared and the ring dropped to the ground, the energy of it drawing her attention. She struggled to her feet, stumbling to where she'd held Castigate.

Gabe reached the spot first, picking up the ring and holding it out to her.

Chapter Thirty

Cassidy stared at the object, half afraid to take it. She could see a faint glow to it and sense the power. Taking the ring from him, she slipped it on her finger. "Why didn't you tell me what'd happen?"

"It was an unwilling binding. Of course he was going to fight it with all the power at his disposal. We're just lucky he wasn't allowed to harm us." He looked down at himself. "Although with the amount of blood coating us that's hard to believe."

Cassidy's gaze returned to the ring she wore. "We did it."

Gabe grinned at her. "Yeah. We did."

Cassidy laughed. "We did it." She threw herself at Gabe, then pulled away when she felt Remedy arrive behind her. She spun, keeping herself between the two of them. "You can't hurt him. I'm allowed to touch him now. We made a deal." She moved forward, stepping out of the salt circle. Gabe followed her and she was tempted to tell him to wait in the circle. "Castigate can't hurt either of us."

"You're lucky you managed with the stunt you pulled earlier. Didn't I tell you not to call me while he still lived? Well?" Remedy looked past her, his eyes narrowing when his gaze landed on Gabe. He pushed her aside and pulled Gabe close, peering intently at him.

Cassidy tried to drag Remedy away from Gabe. "Leave him alone."

Remedy released him, pushed Cassidy away again and swung at Gabe. His fist connected with Gabe's chin. "How dare you," Remedy roared.

Cassidy screamed, throwing herself in front of Remedy, pushing him away from Gabe who'd landed on the ground. "What are you doing? We bound Castigate. What more do you want?"

"He had to get himself caught up in this." Remedy pushed her to the side so he could glare at Gabe, the air around him crackling. "Was that your plan all along?"

Gabe rubbed his chin as he stumbled to his feet. "I wasn't about to let her do this alone."

Cassidy stared at Remedy. "You hit him because he helped me?"

Remedy turned his flame streaked eyes towards Cassidy. "I hit him because eternity will be long enough with one of you. Two is going to make me want to kill. Probably myself."

"You… he… what?" Cassidy turned from one to the other.

Gabe shook his head. "Stop looking at me, I haven't got a clue what's going on."

Remedy grabbed hold of Gabe and shoved him towards Cassidy, one hand on his jaw as he turned his head. "Look at him. Tell me what you see."

Cassidy gazed into Gabe's eyes, her mouth slowly opening. No sound came out. She reached out and touched his face beside his left eye, like he'd done to her so many times. "Gabe." His name was a whisper.

"Cass?" Gabe pushed Remedy's hands away and reached for her. "What's wrong?"

She finally managed to speak. "Fire."

"What? No." Gabe stumbled back from her.

"What's wrong… demon boy?" Remedy's lips twisted into a smile. "It's all right for Cass to be tainted but not you?"

Cassidy could only stare at them, her arms wrapped around herself as she took a step away from Gabe. Was Remedy right?

"No." Gabe reached out for her, stepping forward

when she backed away further. "I didn't mean it like that. I was shocked. I didn't know that'd happen. I don't have a clue how it could have happened."

"You mingled your blood with Cassidy's and Castigate's during the ritual," Remedy said.

Gabe shook his head. "Impossible. I'm not even cut. All the blood on me is Castigate's from when I was helping hold onto him."

Cassidy stared at Gabe, her mouth dropping open. She went to cover it with her right hand, but it fell away when she saw all the blood on it. Her blood, Castigate's blood and the blood she'd accidentally smeared across her palm when she'd applied Gabe's blood to her wrist. "I didn't mean to." She backed away further. "I'm so sorry." She hated those words. "It was when I was putting your blood on my wrist. I didn't know."

Gabe advanced on her as she retreated, eventually managing to wrap his arms around her. "It's okay." He pressed her head against him. "Cass? Talk to me. Please?"

Cassidy lifted her head to stare up at him. "Your family hunt demons. What will they do about us?"

Gabe's lips curved slightly upwards. "Pray for us." He touched her face beside her left eye. "Demon girl, they don't hunt demons, they hunt demons who've done wrong. Sadly most demons tend to do wrong the moment they leave hell."

"What about Remedy? Will they send him to hell?" Cassidy continued to stare into his green eyes, watching the flames that flickered in them.

"We have his true name. You can call him back any time you wish. No sacrifice needed. Now, about our date tomorrow night." He grinned at her.

Cassidy returned his grin as relief rushed through her. "We're not staying home."

He laughed softly. "It was worth a try."

Remedy made a noise of disgust from behind them. "I've got better things to do than stand around watching this sickening display."

"Don't get in trouble with any hunters," Cassidy said.

"Define trouble," Remedy said.

"Like, I don't know, sacrificing virgins or something."

"As if." Remedy started to walk away. "It's rare to find a virgin these days." He disappeared into the shadows of the trees.

Cassidy stared after him. "I'm damned if I know what to do with him half the time. I feel like I should kill him for the part he played in my father's…in…" she still couldn't bring herself to say the word.

Gabe reached out and touched the ring. "You have the true culprit here. Remedy was protecting himself. Demons can't leave alive anyone who knows their true name. It's suicide."

"It's all so confusing."

"Then stop worrying about it. We'll figure it out one day at a time."

"And what if it takes me forever to figure things out?"

Gabe grinned. "Then it's a good thing we have forever."

Cassidy laughed. "Let's go home." She looked down at herself. "I need a shower, this blood's starting to dry." Power still raced through her veins. "But after that, I need to hunt. I just don't think we should be doing it looking like we're actors from a slasher movie."

Gabe nodded as he pulled out his phone and started typing in a message. "Give me a sec then."

"What are you doing? We'll barely have enough daylight left to get in a single hunt. I'll never get to sleep at dawn if I don't use up some of this energy."

"I'm organising someone to come and deal with this blood so it can't be used against us." He tucked his phone away. "Okay. Let's go home." He slid an arm around her waist. "And how about tomorrow you get your motorbike license. We both can."

"I've got my learners. Had it for ages." She pulled away as they reached her motorbike. "I just didn't bother with my P's since it would have taken too long." She glanced around. "What about the weapons we've hidden? Should we collect them?" Although that would probably cut too much into her hunting time. She frowned.

"If the clean up crew doesn't find all of them we can collect them another day. Let's get out of here."

Cassidy slid her helmet on. "Okay." She swung her leg over the motorbike and waited for Gabe to join her before she headed home, going much faster than she should. As Gabe had already pointed out, she had a Remedy for if she was pulled over for speeding. She grinned. And a ring with a demon who had to do her bidding. It would be much more satisfying making Castigate sort it out. When they arrived, Cassidy headed for the bathroom.

"You want me to scrub your back for you?"

"Nice try." She shot him a glance over her shoulder.

"We don't have to worry about interruptions from Remedy anymore."

Cassidy only shook her head, a smile forming as

she closed the bathroom door behind her. She locked the door and moved to the basin to wash her hands. She stared at the painted mirror, several scratches in it. She didn't need the paint anymore. Removing a dagger from her boot, she used the edge of the blade to scrape a large part of the paint away. She stared at herself through the streaky patch.

Flame flecked hazel eyes, reddish brown jagged hair and smears of blood on her face. But the shadows had disappeared from beneath her eyes and the hollow hungry look was gone. Leaving the dagger on the basin, she moved away from the mirror and stripped off her blood soaked clothes before she stepped into the shower.

Maybe next weekend she'd invite Amy over. She might even try and take her clubbing one night. Surely one of her demons could arrange false ID for Amy so she didn't have to wait for her eighteenth birthday that was still several months away. She'd ask Remedy first. No, she'd definitely tell Castigate to arrange it. He would hate that. As she turned the shower off, there was a knock at the bathroom door. "What?"

"If this blood is left to dry any longer I'm going to need to have my clothes surgically removed. Or get help at any rate."

Cassidy finished drying herself and wrapped her towel around her body before she opened the door. "Nice try." She smiled at him. "There's a knife on the basin if you need any help getting your gear off. And don't take too long or I'm leaving without you." She strode to her room to get dressed, her smile widening as she heard Gabe chuckle. Kicking her door shut behind her, she dressed and took out another set of daggers. Heading for the front door, she searched until she located a demon close enough to take on before dawn.

She frowned. There was a demon in her house? A minor one? Turning she watched Gabe walk towards her. Her frown deepened. "You feel like a minor demon."

Gabe reached for her, drawing her close. "So do you. Well, not so minor these days." His lips met hers and his arms tightened around her. Eventually he drew back. "Still going hunting? Or would you like me to help you burn off all that energy some other way?"

Grinning, she pulled away from him, opening the door. "Nice try." She stepped outside, ignoring the sense of demon near her to seek out one she could hunt. The demon she'd noticed before was now a little closer. Which was good since they had less than two hours until dawn. "Let's hunt." She strode to her motorbike and swung her leg over, glancing over her shoulder. "Well? You coming?"

The door was closed behind him and he stood there looking at her, a half smile on his lips. He remained silent a moment longer before he grinned and strode towards her. "Always." He got on behind her, wrapping his arms around her waist as she took off.

Chapter Thirty-One

Cassidy pulled away from Gabe as the song ended. When the nightclub instantly filled with the sound of the next song, she leaned forward to speak into his ear. "Back shortly. Bathroom."

Gabe nodded and pointed to the bar. At his questioning look she nodded before she turned away and headed to the bathroom. She blinked at the brightness in the bathroom after the dim lights of the nightclub. She quickly finished in there and started to leave when she felt a demon arrive in the area. At the end of the corridor was a fire exit. Smearing blood over her demon mark, she slipped through the fire exit quickly enough that the alarm didn't go off, and found herself in an alley behind the nightclub. And there was the demon, fresh blood on him. Human blood.

She stopped mid stride along the alleyway and

planted her hands on her hips. "And don't I just live a perfect fairytale existence. Were you saving this dance for me, Prince Charming?" She was glad now that she hadn't given into the temptation to dress in something other than her usual black jeans and shirt for her night out with Gabe.

The demon stared at her. "I've done nothing against you, sister."

A mirthless smile twisted her mouth. "Now that's where you're wrong. I'm not your sister and your crime against me is harming one of my fellow humans." She drew her daggers from her boots. "Shall we dance?" She felt movement behind her, but after initially tensing, she realised it was Gabe.

"Dancing with other guys already? We have an eternity and you're already bored with me?"

"I'll save you a dance, but this one is his." She sent him a glance as he came to a stop beside her. "And I'm not sharing."

Gabe waved her forward. "Go ahead. I love watching you fight, demon girl." He grinned and lowered his voice. "It gives me all sorts of ideas."

"Huh. You get ideas just breathing." She turned her attention to the demon that was backing away. "Oh no you don't." She leapt forward, her daggers flashing through the air, both striking their target. "You're not welcome on Earth. Go to hell where you belong."

The demon fought back, but he was only a minor one and no match for her. Several times he tried to escape. She was too quick for him, blocking the attempt each time. He also pleaded with her to let him go, that he wouldn't hurt another human. She didn't believe him.

The fight was over quicker than she expected and she turned to Gabe, energy still humming in her veins as she slid her daggers back into her boots. She scowled. "He could have put up more of a fight. Now I'm left with heaps of energy."

"I've got a suggestion for that."

"Nice try. Let's hunt."

Gabe grinned. "That'll work too. So much for a night out. We didn't even get to have a drink." He slid an arm around her waist and walked with her to the front of the nightclub where her motorbike was parked. When they were nearly there, he stopped. "Wait here." When she nodded, he strode towards a woman carrying a basket of individually wrapped, long stemmed roses.

Cassidy watched as he pulled out his wallet and bought a single red rose. When he returned to her side, she gestured towards the wallet. "When did you get that?"

"My family returned it and my ID this arve when they dropped off all our weapons. I guess they figured I'm a hopeless cause." He held the rose out to her. "It might not be blood, but I'm hoping you like it better."

Cassidy laughed as she took the rose. "I don't think it was being a hopeless cause. It was probably your stubbornness that got through to them." She stepped close to him. "It tends to have a wearing effect." She pressed her lips against his, one arm holding him close.

Gabe kissed her, his hands splayed on her back. He finally drew away slightly. "Stubborn? I think you could teach me a thing or two about that." He grinned. "If we're going hunting we better head now before I try and convince you we should go home."

"We'll get home eventually." She reached up and touched his face lightly beside his left eye. "Demon boy."

"Eventually. Sounds good to me." He reached for his helmet. "Let's hunt so we can go home."

Cassidy grinned as she took her helmet off the handlebar, tucking her rose down the side of her boot, beside one of her daggers. "Sounds like a plan to me." She hopped on her motorbike and waited until Gabe's arms were wrapped around her before she took off, heading for the nearest demon. It wasn't a minor one. Energy sang through her veins and she hoped he was causing trouble. Because she needed to hunt and he felt like he might be enough of a challenge for them. Although he wasn't enough of a challenge to warrant ordering Castigate to fight with them. She was looking forward to that moment. He would hate every second of it. She pulled up in front of a park that was full of large trees and plenty of shadows, getting off the motorbike as soon as Gabe hopped off.

"Now remember, no attacking him unless he's up to no good," Gabe said.

Before she could answer, a scream broke the silence of the night and, grinning, Cassidy dropped her helmet to the ground. "It sounds like he's up to no good to me."

Drawing her daggers she ran towards the demon she could sense in the darkest section of the park, Gabe at her side, energy coursing through her body. It was time to hunt. There was a demon that needed to be returned to hell.

Free Ebook

Subscribe to Avril's newsletter to receive a free ebook. This ebook is exclusive to those on her mailing list. To find out more about this offer visit: http://www.avrilsabine.com/free-ebook/

*

We value your privacy and will not sell, rent, exchange or loan your email address to third parties. Your information is confidential and you are under no obligation to remain on the mailing list and can unsubscribe at any time.

Acknowledgements

Thank you. Not only to my beta readers and editors who helped make this a better story, but also to my readers for all their positive feedback about the other books in the series.

To The Reader

If you enjoyed this book, why not consider leaving a review to help other readers discover it too? Reader engagement is one of the few ways that lets an author know readers want more books in a particular series or genre. So leave a review and tell friends, not only about this book but also about other ones you've enjoyed, so you can continue to enjoy books by your favourite authors for years to come.

Dreams are meant to be lived,

Avril.

About The Author

Avril is an Australian author who lives with her family on acreage in South East Queensland. She writes mostly young adult speculative fiction, but has been known to dabble in other genres. You can find more information about her at her website www.avrilsabine.com where you can also subscribe to her newsletter to be kept informed about new releases, current projects, blog posts and exclusive news.

Titles By Avril Sabine

Stories about strong characters and characters who discover their strengths.

SERIES

Assassins Of The Dead- Young Adult Fantasy/ Paranormal

Book 1: Dark Blade

Book 2: Dragon Touched

Book 3: Society Against Vampires

Book 4: King's Request

Dragon Blood- Young Adult Urban Fantasy (with elements of romance)

(5 book series)

Book 1: Pliethin

Book 2: Wyvern

Book 3: Surety

Book 4: Knight

Book 5: Mage

Dragon Mage- Young Adult Urban Fantasy (with elements of romance)

(Series two of Dragon Blood series)

Book 1: Promise

Dragon Blood Chronicles- Young Adult Urban Fantasy (with elements of romance)

(Companion stand alone series to Dragon Blood)

Book 1: Oath

Book 2: Betrayed

Guardians Of The Round Table- Young Adult Fantasy LitRPG

(Co-written with Storm and Rhys Petersen)

Book 1: Dexterity Fail

Book 2: Goblin Boots

Book 3: Singed Feathers

Book 4: Frog Mage

Book 5: Crystal Mine

Book 6: Cursed Harp

Rosie's Rangers- Young Adult Western Steampunk

(6 book series)

Book 1: Justice

Book 2: Vengeance

Book 3: Treachery

Book 4: Accused

Book 5: Wanted

Book 6: Corruption

Mark Of Kings- Children's Fantasy

(Upper middle grade/preteen)

(4 book series)

Book 1: The Arena

Book 2: The Island

Book 3: The Assassin

Book 4: The King

STAND ALONE SERIES

*Demon Hunters- Young Adult Urban Fantasy/
Horror (with elements of romance)*

Book 1: Blood Sacrifice

Book 2: Retribution

Book 3: Tainted

Book 4: Premonition

Book 5: Cursed

Book 6: Feud

Book 7: Extrication

Plea Of The Damned- Young Adult Urban Fantasy/Paranormal

(6 book series)

Book 1: Forgive Me Lucy

Book 2: Forgive Me Aiden

Book 3: Forgive Me Jena

Book 4: Forgive Me Kobe

Book 5: Forgive Me Marti

Book 6: Forgive Me Dawson

Realms Of The Fae- Young Adult Urban Fantasy
(with elements of romance)

The Sword (short story in Like A Girl Anthology)

Heart Of Stone

Book 1: A Debt Owed

Book 2: Marked By The Hunt

Book 3: The Magic Collector

Book 4: An Unexpected Betrayal

Book 5: Imprisoned By Iron

Fairytales Retold (Short Stories)

Snow-White And Rose-Red

The Twelve Brothers

The Light Princess

Beauty And The Beast

Sleeping Beauty

Aschenputtel

The Golden Bird

The Frog Prince

The Death Of Koshchei The Deathless

Myths And Legends Retold (Short Stories)

Ion, Son Of Apollo

Sir Gawain And The Maid With The Narrow Sleeves

Princess Ilse, The Giant's Daughter

YOUNG ADULT NOVELS

Young Adult Fantasy (with elements of romance)

Elf Sight

Earth Bound

Young Adult Urban Fantasy

Stone Warrior (with elements of romance)

The Jungle Inside

Young Adult Contemporary (with elements of romance)

Through Your Eyes

The Ugly Stepsister

Perfect Little Princess

Young Adult Contemporary/Paranormal

Whispers In The Dark (with elements of romance and same sex relationships)

Over Too Soon (with elements of romance)

Young Adult Sci-Fi

Experiment X-One-Six (Urban Sci-Fi/Superheroes)

An Endless Dawn (Post Apocalyptic Sci-Fi)

CHILDREN'S BOOKS

Dragon Lord (Preteen/early teens) (Fantasy)

The Irish Wizard (Upper middle grade) (Urban Fantasy)

SHORT STORIES

Urban Fantasy

Eternally Late

Dealings With Joe

Glimpses (short story in That Moment When Anthology)

Contemporary

The Brat Next Door

Fantasy LitRPG

(Set in the same world as Guardians Of The Round Table Series)

Tales Of Inadon 1: The Disc (Co-written with Storm and Rhys Petersen) (short story in Game On! Anthology)

Post Apocalyptic Sci-Fi

Compulsive Directive

NONFICTION

A Year Of Weekly Writing Exercises (Creative Writing)

Cooking For Families With Allergies (Cooking) (Co-written with Storm Petersen)

Tell Me A Story, Grandma (Memoir)

For the most up to date details on available titles visit:

www.avrilsabine.com/books/bibliography

Demon Hunters Series

To learn more about this series visit:

www.avrilsabine.com/series/dh

BOOKS AVAILABLE IN THE DEMON HUNTER SERIES

Book 1: Blood Sacrifice

Book 2: Retribution

Book 3: Tainted

Book 4: Premonition

Book 5: Cursed

Book 6: Feud

Book 7: Extrication

Disclaimer

This is a work of fiction. Names, characters, businesses, places, events and incidents are either the products of the author's imagination or used in a fictitious manner. Any resemblance to actual persons, living or dead, or actual events is purely coincidental. The opinions expressed or beliefs held are those of the characters and should not be assumed to be the opinions or beliefs of the author.

www.ingramcontent.com/pod-product-compliance
Lightning Source LLC
Chambersburg PA
CBHW050804190726
48285CB00005B/1783